ALL POINTS OF LIGHT CONVERGE

A NOVEL IN STORIES

BY BETH BURGMEYER

For information contact:
Unsolicited Press
Portland, Oregon
www.unsolicitedpress.com
orders@unsolicitedpress.com
619-354-8005

Cover Design: Kathryn Gerhardt
Editor: Summer Stewart

ISBN: 978-1-963115-16-1

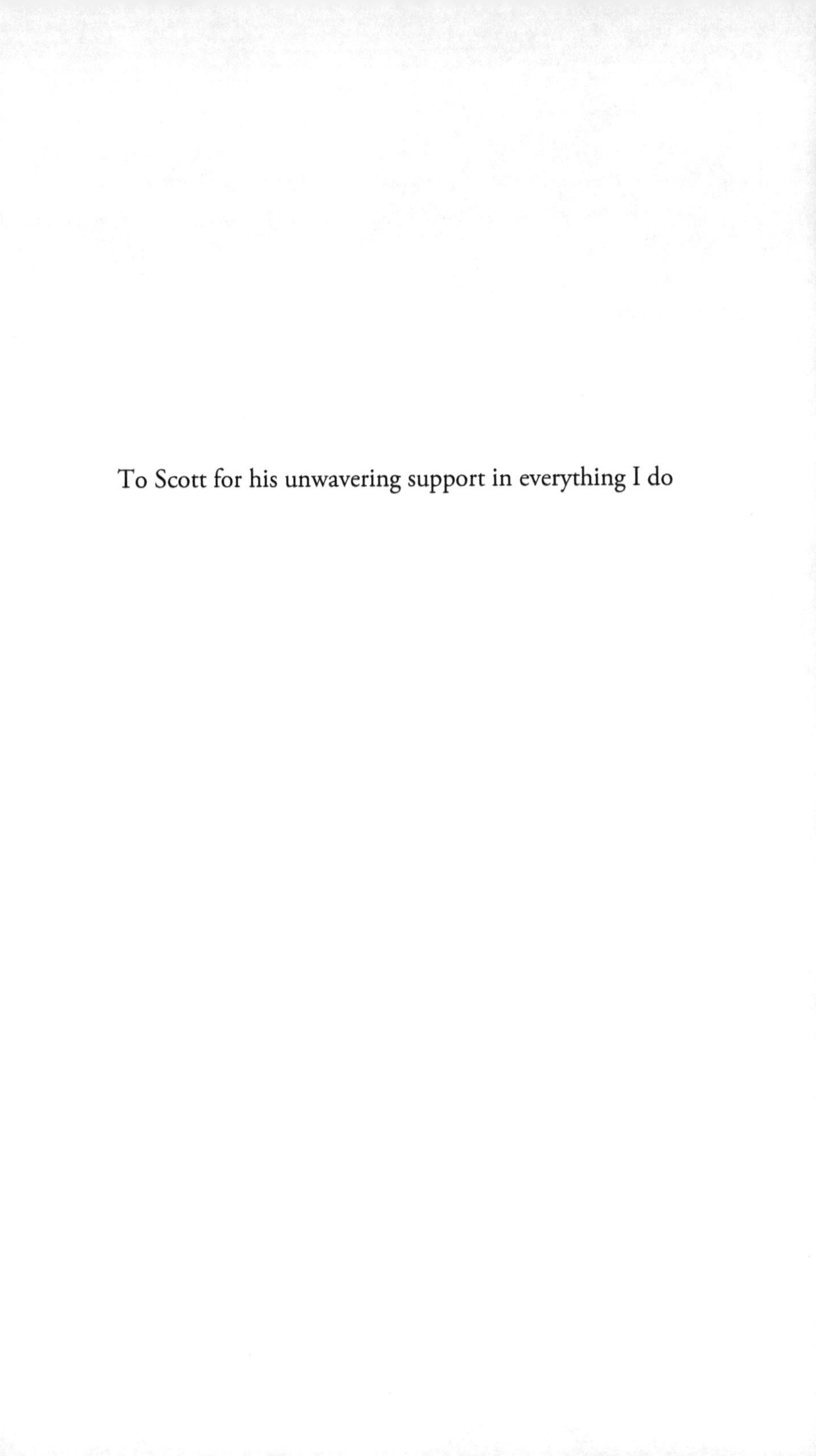

To Scott for his unwavering support in everything I do

ALL POINTS OF
LIGHT CONVERGE

FREEDOM ROAD

Kita sat in her car and stared at the duffel bag, pillow, and backpack that were splayed across the passenger seat. The silent, inanimate passengers stared back like they were daring her to go, to take them somewhere, anywhere but here. She glanced at the hotel across the street, a whole twenty miles from her house. Twenty miles wasn't enough. Two hundred might not even be enough.

"Twenty miles is a start," she whispered to the air around her. The famous Lao Tzu quote went through her head as she stepped out of the car: *The journey of a thousand miles begins with one step.* The first step was the grocery store in front of her. Then the hotel, where she could sit and think, try to figure out a plan. Right now she just needed to put one foot in front of the other.

It was strange to walk through the grocery store without a list, without thinking about what John would want to eat for the week, what Georgia would want if she came home for the weekend. Not that she'd be coming home this weekend, unless John went to pick her up from jail.

It had been Georgia's voice on the phone at two o'clock this afternoon that pushed Kita to pack her things, to drive twenty miles west on Interstate 80 with no clue as to where she was going.

"Mom?" Georgia's tearful voice had come through the phone while Kita sat at the kitchen table drinking a glass of water after her five-mile run.

Kita's pulse quickened while her heart dove into her stomach. "What's wrong?" She wondered how many more *wrongs* she could take when it came to her nineteen-year-old daughter.

"I'm—I'm in jail," she sobbed.

Kita stood up. "Jail?" Jail was a new one. "Why are you—? What for?"

Silence answered her. Finally, Georgia replied, her voice holding an edge of irritation. "For drunk and disorderly, but it was stupid, I wasn't—"

Kita had learned to expect bad news from Georgia, or about Georgia. This past year had been a nightmare—academic probation, parties in the dorms, failing classes. But not this. Not jail. "You were drunk during the day? What were you thinking?!"

"I wasn't that drunk, Mom." Georgia's earlier sobs were replaced by the steely voice Kita knew so well. "You need to come and get me," she ordered.

Something clicked like a switch inside of Kita. All the bottled fear, anger, helplessness, morphed into nothing. Numb nothingness. An exhausted numbness that made her sit back down, made her realize she couldn't do it anymore. She didn't have any more rescues left inside her.

"No," she said in a voice she didn't recognize. A dead voice.

"What? What do you mean, no?" Georgia demanded. "Mom, you have to come and get me!"

Kita hung up and set her phone on the table.

The numbness accompanied her while she crammed as many clothes as possible into her duffel bag. She'd grabbed some of her art supplies too, although she didn't know why. They'd been untouched for years, remnants of a life that didn't seem like hers.

The numbness persisted while she walked the aisles of the grocery store, while she politely answered the check-out person's questions in the right way. Yes, she'd found everything she was looking for. Lie. Yes, she was doing just fine on this beautiful summer day. Bigger lie.

It truly was a beautiful summer day, cooler than usual on a late June afternoon in Iowa. A sweet wind met her when she walked through the automatic doors to the parking lot, waking her up, blowing through the cracks in her numb cocoon.

The sight of the old school bus haphazardly parked next to her car momentarily distracted her from Georgia and John and her life. She couldn't recall ever seeing a bus like it in Des Moines. The classic yellow and black paint was replaced by a dark green that was covered with graffiti art. Some of the artwork was beautiful, while some was sloppy and childlike.

Kita walked around her car and took a closer look at the bus. On the side closest to her car, the words FREEDOM ROAD were painted in bold rainbow colors running the length of the bus. Below that in different lettering, someone had spray painted, *your destination station.*

She wandered around to the back of the bus where the words *Lovin' You* were painted across the back door in what was probably once bright blue paint that was now faded and chipped. The other side of the bus was covered in a hodgepodge of people's names, cities, states, and the names of some mountains and mountain ranges.

Mount Shasta caught Kita's eye. She froze, placing her hand on her chest, clutching the invisible breath she'd just sucked in and held. That breath held a different lifetime, a path that would have taken her far from the Midwest. Far from everything ordinary.

Tears blurred her vision as she turned to go back to her car. Kita had just come around the back of the bus when she saw the young woman a second too late. They hit each other at full force, sending both of them and their grocery bags sprawling on the ground.

"Oh, god, I'm so sorry," Kita said, looking at the young woman who had dirty blonde dreadlocks that fell almost to her waist.

The young woman's face shifted from startled to amused. Laughter erupted from her throat. A long, free, musical laugh.

A young guy with a curly black beard jogged up and knelt beside the woman. "Whoa, everybody okay?" He leaned forward to grab an apple that was rolling away, giving Kita a whiff of body odor. The guy and his clothes looked like they hadn't been washed in weeks.

"That was…" the girl giggled, "that was a trip."

Kita looked at the two bedraggled kids in front of her and the groceries all over the ground. Like everything else in her life, it was chaos. She got to her knees and tried to scoop up her groceries, but tears stung her eyes again. Why did everything have to be so hard?

"I'm sorry," Kita said again. "I was just looking—I mean, I didn't see you." She swiped at her eyes, wondering if her cheeks were as red as they felt.

The guy reached out and touched her arm. "Hey, pretty lady. Why so sad?"

She would have laughed if she wasn't so flustered. Pretty was the last word she'd use to describe herself. She was still in her jogging shorts and shirt, her limp black hair pulled back in a ponytail. There was no make up to cover the bags under her eyes, the bags that made her look fifty instead of thirty-six.

"It's nothing," Kita said. She turned her attention back to the girl. "Are you sure you're okay?" The girl didn't look much older than Georgia, possibly even younger.

"I'm good," the girl answered as she picked up some of the groceries and put them back in her worn cloth bag. "No worries."

No worries. Kita wished she had no worries. If she had no worries, she wouldn't be leaving, she wouldn't be sitting on her ass in a parking lot next to some psychedelic bus talking to two kids who looked like they hadn't seen the inside of a shower for a long time.

Kita tried to sort through the groceries on the ground. One of her paper bags had ripped and she had no idea how to get everything into one bag. She should just offer the food to the guy and girl. They looked like they needed it more than she did. She could go back to the store and get more. But she didn't want to insult them. If she talked to them, got to know them a little, they might accept the food from her.

Kita stood, giving up on the groceries for the moment. "I was, um, I was just looking at your bus," Kita said. "It's nice. I like the artwork."

"Oh it's not ours. It's Nate's," the girl said, throwing her head in the direction of the grocery store. "He's still in there. Takes him a real long time to shop. I guess he's what you'd call a deliberate shopper. Or is it an intentional shopper?" She looked to the guy for an answer.

"Yeah, Nate's a pretty intentional guy." He said it as though he'd just said something profound. "He's a good guy though. A little too serious, but, hey, everybody's got their own load to bear."

"Yeah, they do," Kita mumbled. The guy was profound after all.

"Nate picked us up outside of Chicago," the guy said. "We were flying a sign, hoping to get to Utah for the gathering. Nate saw us and here we are."

Kita didn't understand half of what he'd just said. "Yeah, here we are," she echoed. She shifted her weight. "Since you're traveling, do you want these?" Kita motioned to the groceries, hoping she sounded casual, not condescending.

"Really?" the girl asked, her eyes brightening. "You sure?"

"Yeah, I'm sure. If my daughter was on the road, I'd want people to help her." *The road.* Kita had longed for the road once, had planned a whole summer on the road. A summer that unexpectedly turned into morning sickness and a shotgun wedding. She took a different road, a different life. Not her life.

"Thanks for the food," the guy said. He held out his hand. "I'm Sonny." He glanced at the girl. "This is Ripple."

Kita took Sonny's hand. "I'm Kita."

Ripple stepped forward and put her arms around Kita. "Thanks, sweet sister."

Kita gave her a sad smile. "It's the least I can do for knocking you down."

"You want to come on the bus and eat with us?" Ripple asked.

"Yeah, Nate won't mind," Sonny said.

Before Kita could answer, Sonny looked over her head and called out, "Nate!" His voice rang with joy, like he'd just seen a long-lost friend.

Kita turned to see a tall, lean guy walk their way. He had shaggy, dark brown hair that couldn't really be called long or short. Although his khaki shorts were threadbare in parts and his shirt had a few holes, he looked like he'd seen a shower in the last day or two. As he neared them, she could tell he was older than Sonny and Ripple, but not as old as she was.

Nate walked over and gave Kita a questioning look. She imagined the picture the four of them must have made standing beside the bus. She was acutely aware she didn't belong in the small huddle.

"This is Kita," Ripple said, latching on to Kita's arm. It was so different from the way Georgia was with her now. Whenever they were in public together, Georgia acted like Kita had the plague. Any sign of affection—a hand on her daughter's shoulder, a hug—was quickly rebuked.

"Hey, Kita," Nate said. He smiled, but it wasn't the free kind of smile Ripple and Sonny had given her.

"Hi." She shifted her weight back and forth, trying to figure out how to make an exit. "I, um, I just ran into Ripple. I mean, literally ran into her. I was looking at your bus and I wasn't looking where I was going and…" She shook her head, wishing her cheeks weren't burning.

"Look." Ripple pointed to the mess of groceries. "She gave us some food too."

"Thanks," Nate said. "That was nice."

Kita bent down and tried to stuff more food in the already overflowing paper bag. Sonny grabbed some of the remaining food, trying to balance it in his arms.

"Yeah, we invited her on the bus to eat with us," Sonny said.

"I, well, I don't think I can stay, but I'll at least help you get these inside," Kita said. A part of her longed for just a little companionship, even from strangers. Lately she realized just how isolated she'd been, how alone she'd been, especially now with the way things were with Georgia.

If John were there he'd tell her she was stupid for getting into a vehicle with three strangers. They could be kidnappers or serial killers. As she followed the three of them up the stairs and onto the bus, the little rush of adrenaline from doing something risky made her feel alive for the first time in years.

Kita was surprised by how homey the inside of the bus was. There were still a few original bus seats, but most of the bus had been redone. Some countertops and cabinets were built in toward the front of the bus along with a small refrigerator and stove top. Long rows of cabinets lined each side of the bus above the seats and benches. Some of the benches could double for beds. A makeshift twin bed was built into the back of the bus.

"This is really nice," Kita said.

"Thanks," Nate said. "It's home for now."

A pang of envy passed through Kita. What would it be like to have that kind of freedom?

She stood back while the three of them put most of the food away. Ripple kept out some bread, peanut butter, jelly, and some of the fruit Kita had given them.

Kita told herself to get off the bus, to get on with her plan—not that she could really call it a plan at this point—but she needed to move, or at least figure out where she was going. Instead of leaving, she leaned against a cabinet. "Where did you say you were headed?" she asked.

"To the Rainbow Gathering in Utah," Ripple said.

Kita imagined a big LGBTQ rally, but Utah didn't seem like the place for something like that. "Why Utah?"

"It's in a different national forest every year," Sonny said.

"Forest?" Kita was lost.

Ripple laughed. Something about her free, untainted laughter made Kita wish she could grasp it and hold onto it for the dark moments in her life. "You don't know what we're talking about, do you."

Kita shook her head. "I thought rainbow stood for—"

"This is a different rainbow," Ripple said. "I'd try to tell you what it's about, but I can't. You just gotta go experience it yourself."

Nate pulled out some plates and looked at Kita. "People from all over the country go. We all gather in the forest for a week, thousands of us." He got a faraway look in his eyes. "There's nothing else like it. It's like coming home."

Home. Kita had no idea what that word meant anymore. There was nowhere she felt at home. Especially since her grandma died.

"It sounds nice," Kita said. She glanced over her shoulder at the bus door. "Well, I should probably go."

"You going home?" Sonny asked.

Kita looked out the window toward the hotel, then in the direction of the interstate. "No, not home. I just need to go somewhere. Anywhere but here." Her face burned from saying too much.

Nate quietly studied her, making her wonder what he was thinking.

"It was nice to meet all of you," Kita said. "I hope—"

"Hey!" Ripple said, her eyes growing big and bright. "You wanna come with us? I mean if you're not going home and you're just gonna go somewhere, you might as well come with us to the gathering."

Although Kita envied their carefree lifestyle, she wasn't about to do something that crazy. "I can't—I don't—I don't even know you."

"Sure you do," Sonny said. "This is us. This is Ripple and me and Nate. What you see is what you get. We're picking up some more people as we go. It'll be great."

The thought of adventure grabbed her for just a moment, but she wasn't like them. She wasn't young and free, unattached. "Thanks, but I can't."

Sonny put his arm around Ripple and looked at Kita with a wisdom that surprised her. "You look like you could use a break from this shitty world for a while. Like Ripple said, if you need someplace to go, there's no place better. You'll be loved, you'll be fed. You won't meet better people."

"It sounds great, but—"

"But you said you don't have anywhere to go," Ripple said, her voice deflating, her shoulders drooping.

"Ripple, it's okay," Nate said in a gentle voice. "She said she can't go." He turned to Kita. "Thanks a lot for the food. Most people aren't that nice."

Kita nodded. "You're welcome. It was nice to talk to all of you. Have fun at your gathering."

Ripple and Sonny both hugged her at the same time. Ripple's hair and Sonny's beard scratched her face. She held her breath for a moment, unsure if she could handle that much body odor at once.

"Blessings," Ripple said as she pulled away from Kita.

"Safe travels," Sonny added.

When she walked down the steps and out the bus door she felt as deflated as Ripple looked. She'd only taken a few steps toward her car when Nate's voice stopped her.

"Hey, Kita." He leaned back against the bus, blocking the O and the M on FREEDOM, leaving the word, FREED.

Freed, she wanted to be freed. Needed to be freed. Despite that desire, she stayed rooted in her spot.

"We'll be here for a little while if you change your mind." He looked down for a moment, then back at her. "I'm not trying to put pressure on you or anything. Just wanted to let you know."

"Thanks," she said, noticing just how blue his eyes were. When was the last time she noticed John's eyes? *Shut up*, she admonished herself. It was stupid to stand there looking into some stranger's eyes. A guy who looked like he was a few years out of college. "I think I need to go my own way. Wherever that might be."

Nate cocked his head at her. "We're all going somewhere. Even if you're lost, you're going somewhere."

"And what if you're stuck," Kita said before she could stop herself. "What if you've been standing in one place for nineteen years."

Nate gave her a half smile. "You're not standing still anymore."

She shrugged. "No, I guess not."

Nate stayed in his spot, leaning against the bus while Kita got into her car.

She backed out of her parking spot and drove toward the hotel, taking one last glance at the FREEDOM ROAD in her rearview mirror.

##

Kita sat in her parked car near the entrance of the hotel, had sat there for almost thirty minutes. Stuck. Should she go in and get a room? Should she text John and let him know she was leaving? Let him know about Georgia? Texting was the coward's way out, but she didn't feel very brave at the moment.

The loud ping from her phone alerted her to a text.

John's name and message appeared on the screen: *Where are you?*

Kita glanced at the time. He hadn't been home this early in months. Whatever affair he'd had this time might be over. Or his mistress wasn't available tonight. Was it strange that she didn't care anymore?

I don't know, she sent back to him. It was true. She had no idea where she was, where the real Kita was, where she'd gone. She wasn't Kita anymore, the free-spirited girl who was headed to Columbia University on an art scholarship. That Kita got lost when she got pregnant just before her seventeenth birthday, when she and John got married because it was the right thing to do for the baby. Now that baby sat in a jail cell throwing away her chance at college, a chance Kita would have given anything for.

Kita jumped when her phone rang. John's name appeared on her screen.

"Hi," she said. The numbness returned to her head, traveling down to her heart.

"Are you okay?" It was the first time in a long time he'd sounded concerned about her. "What do you mean you don't know where you are? Is everything okay? You need me to come and get you?"

"No."

"No, what?" he asked. "No you're not okay, or no you don't need me to come and get you?"

"Yes." The numbness spread to her voice. "I mean, no, don't come and get me."

"What in the hell's going on?" The hint of frustration was all too familiar.

"I have to leave. Just for a little while. I can't do it anymore. I can't take anymore from Georgia."

"What happened now?" Exasperation pulsed through her phone.

"She's in jail. Drunk and disorderly."

"Shit," he muttered. "God dammit!" Louder. "Well are you headed to get her?"

"No, I'm not getting her." Years of resentment, of feeling like a single parent, bubbled inside her like lava. "If you want her out of jail, you can go get her. You're the big shot lawyer. Or just let her sit there and serve her time."

"You're just leaving? In the middle of a crisis, you're leaving?! You can't do that. I have a job, I don't have time for this shit. You need to get home now."

"I can't, I'm so tired, I just—"

"And you don't think I'm tired!" he bellowed. "Do you have any idea—"

Kita hung up and turned her phone to vibrate.

She'd held onto a tiny splinter of hope that he'd understand, that he'd acknowledge her pain, her struggle. It might have been the lifeline she needed to pull her back home. But that splinter of hope disintegrated into sawdust.

Her phone vibrated. John again.

She tossed her phone in the passenger's seat and glanced across the street at the grocery store. A gas station and a few trees obscured her view of the parking lot.

Kita started her car, trying not to think about the insane thing she was about to do. Maybe they wouldn't be there anymore. It would be best if they'd already left because it was truly crazy to get on an old bus with people she didn't know, headed someplace she knew nothing about.

When she didn't see the bus in the parking lot, she should have been relieved. The choice had been taken away from her. Now she could do something saner, like drive to Lincoln and stay for a week or two. Or more. She could drive by Gram's old house, go to all the familiar restaurants and shops they went to during Kita's summers with her grandma.

Instead of relief, a heavy stone of regret fell into her stomach. The chance to unearth that impulsive, adventurous soul that used to live inside of her had already driven away.

She turned her car in the direction of another gas station on the far side of the grocery store parking lot. She needed to fill her tank before heading to Lincoln.

The weight in her stomach was replaced by a thousand winged butterflies when she saw the FREEDOM ROAD at the gas station. Nate stood outside, leaning against the bus while he filled the gas tank.

It took less than a minute for her to reach the gas station and get out of her car.

Nate gave her a quizzical smile as she walked toward him.

"Can I go with you?" She wondered if he heard the tremor in her voice.

"You sure?" he asked.

She wasn't sure, but she nodded. "If it's still okay."

Before Nate could answer, Ripple flew out the bus door and enveloped Kita in a bear hug. "Of course it's okay." She turned her head toward an open window at the back of the bus. "Kita's coming!"

Sonny stuck his head out the open window. "Perfect," he said, grinning at her.

Kita stood there for a moment, realizing she felt more wanted by strangers than her own family.

"I, uh, I just need to grab my stuff from my car and park it somewhere. I can have my—" She almost said husband but stopped herself. He hadn't been her husband for years. Not really. They were roommates who barely tolerated each other. "I can have someone pick it up for me."

Kita picked a parking spot near the gas station, then grabbed her duffel bag, backpack, and the little travel pillow that used to be Gram's. The summer wind blew against her as she walked toward the bus. She closed her eyes and inhaled freedom.

##

Kita woke to the sound of rain pelting against the bus window. A light blanket covered her on the long, cushioned bench. Someone must have covered her after she'd fallen asleep. It took a few moments to orient herself, to remember what she'd done. She sat up and looked out the window at a rest area parking lot. The rainclouds obscured the light, making it impossible to tell what time of day it was. She grabbed her phone. Along with a barrage of texts from John, the screen showed it was just past 6:30 a.m.

Twelve hours ago she'd been sitting in a hotel parking lot, deciding to do something insane. Something no thirty-six-year-old suburban mother did. Now she was on a bus with three strangers headed to Utah. She looked down at her hands, her legs, her feet. No, it was four strangers.

A quick glance around showed Sonny and Ripple asleep, their bodies entwined beneath some blankets on the twin bed at the back of the old, converted school bus. Nate wasn't on the bus.

Kita grabbed her little toiletry bag and headed to the bathroom. After she peed, she washed her hands and face, the icy water waking her up. She pulled her hair free from the messy ponytail and brushed it before pulling it back again. She put on deodorant, wondering when she'd get the chance to take a shower.

She wanted a shower.

She wanted hot coffee.

She wanted her whole grain oatmeal, the morning news, the comfort of a soft couch, a bathroom that smelled and looked clean. A familiar, heavenly bed that cradled her, a bed she could crawl into and go back to sleep.

When she saw her ragged expression in the splotchy, rusted mirror, she did a double take. Her olive complexion looked washed out, her dark brown eyes were swallowed by bags. Getting on the bus yesterday was a mistake. She'd planned to stay at a hotel somewhere for a while, not live on a bus. She didn't even have a blanket or food. She wasn't prepared for something like this. The reality of what she'd done made her so nauseous, she fought the urge to throw up.

Kita rushed from the bathroom and into the rain. Instead of heading to the bus, she ran up the hill to a picnic table that was sheltered by the massive branches of an old oak tree. There, she buried her head in her hands and cried while droplets of rain fell from the umbrella of leaves, dotting her T-shirt like splatters of paint.

"Kita?"

She hadn't heard Nate walk up the hill. She looked up and wondered if he thought it was a mistake to bring her along. It was clear that she didn't belong, that she wasn't cut out for it.

He sat beside her on the top of the picnic table.

"Where are we?" she asked. If by some miracle they were close enough to Des Moines, John might come and get her. The thought made her want to throw up again. Not John. Her cousin, Janice, might come. They weren't close, but Janice was nice. A nice Christian who would pick her up because it was the right thing to do.

"Near Ogallala."

"Shit." Kita bowed her head. Ogallala was a seven-hour drive from Des Moines. Even Janice wasn't Christian enough to drive that far.

"You okay?" Genuine concern flavored Nate's question.

She looked up at him, hoping those blue eyes would hold some magic answer. "This was a mistake. I—I shouldn't be here. I never should have done this. God, what was I thinking?"

"You want to go home?"

She expected some sort of judgement from him, but it was just a simple question. But it wasn't a simple question. John's angry voice messages, his text messages that screamed in all capital letters played through her head.

"No I don't want to go home," she conceded. "God, I can't go back, not right now. But this—this is crazy. I can't do this. I don't even know you. I don't even know what this rainbow thing is. I was just going to spend a week or two in a hotel, hang out in Lincoln. I can't—I don't have anything with me. I gave all my food to Ripple and Sonny. I don't even have a blanket. I don't know where or when I'll get coffee or breakfast or a shower."

He silently studied her, making her wonder what he was thinking.

"I get it," he said. "I've been there. More than once."

"What do you mean?" He seemed pretty comfortable on his old bus, picking up strangers, living a nomadic life.

"I've been there. Living a life you thought you wanted but really didn't. And I've been stuck, but not just stuck. Terrified."

He gave a name to the nauseous weight in her stomach. Fear. She was scared to death. "Yeah, I really don't have any business being out here." She hated herself for failing at one more thing.

Nate shrugged. "You have as much business being out here as I do, but if you really want to go back, I'll try to find you a ride or get you to a bus station or airport. However you want to travel."

She expected the relief that swathed her, but not the twinge of disappointment. "You know, I was going to do this the summer I was seventeen," she said. "I bought an old van. My best friend and I were going to live in it, head out to San Francisco, check out Berkley. Then we were going to drive up the coast and go see Mount Shasta. But, now..." She shook her head. "I'm not cut out for this anymore. As much as I hate to admit it, you're right. I'm stuck and I'm scared. Terrified."

Nate looked down at his clasped hands, his fingers fidgety as if he was uncomfortable. "Believe it or not, I really do get it. Being terrified, frozen with fear halfway up the mountain. If you go back, you failed. But you don't know if you have the energy or the courage to keep going." He looked down at the picnic table bench. "And whatever's up there, the shit you can't see, the shit that might kill you. It paralyzes you."

Somehow he put into words exactly how she felt. It made her wonder what had happened to him.

"If I go back..." Images of Georgia went through her head—her daughter's eyes and words that spit acid at Kita. Loneliness. An invisible solitary confinement. That's what waited for her at home. Her little bedroom down the hall from where John slept. The empty, cold, beautiful house. "I can't go back, but..." She had no idea how to finish the sentence.

Nate cocked his head at her. "You can go anywhere you want to go."

Kita looked up to see Ripple running up the hill, her dreadlocks bouncing, her skirt flowing behind her.

"Coffee's ready," she said as if coffee were gold. She climbed onto the table and put her arm around Kita. "Isn't the rain great?"

She looked at Ripple, who sounded like a sweet kid, and at Nate who somehow, on some level, understood her fear, understood the impasse she was at. She impulsively gave Ripple a hug, not caring how bad the girl smelled. "It is great," she said. "Coffee sounds even better."

The left side of Nate's mouth curved into a half smile. "So you're coming with us?" he asked.

"I think so."

Ripple grabbed her hand. "Of course she is."

Kita stepped onto the bus and inhaled the rich smell of fresh coffee. Nate grabbed some coffee mugs from one of the upper cabinets. Sonny got out some of the milk, fruit, and cheese that Kita had given them yesterday.

Ripple held her coffee cup up as if giving a toast. "Here's to a beautiful morning and beautiful people. Thanks for the breakfast, Kita."

"Hell yeah," Sonny added.

The coffee was strong, but there was something about it that made it the best cup of coffee Kita had ever tasted.

They'd been on the road for about an hour when Kita pulled her sketch book and pencils from her backpack. It was a blank sketchbook she'd gotten back when Georgia started kindergarten. She was so sure she'd be able to get back into art, hone her skills again, even take some classes at the community college. But there was a never-ending supply of laundry, housework, cooking…exhaustion. The artist suffocated, leaving a mother and wife in its place. The last picture she'd sketched was of Georgia when she was a newborn, napping, swaddled in her blanket. Her sweet face had been the picture of peace and innocence and beauty. It hung in Georgia's bedroom, but Kita wondered if she even saw it anymore.

She looked at the empty sketchbook, then at Nate who was sitting diagonal from her, giving her a profiled view of his face as he drove. His face looked intense, his eyes on the road, but there seemed to be more etched on his face than concentration. There was something both mellow and intense about him. Kita tried to capture that duality as she sketched him.

At first it felt awkward, unnatural to sketch, to try to bring something to life on a flat, blank space. What if she'd lost any semblance of talent? She told herself to shut up. She wasn't working on some masterpiece; she wasn't preparing for an art show. She was just drawing a picture of a guy driving a bus. Once she let go of expectations, gave herself permission to just draw, tendrils of joy traveled from her pencil into her body.

She'd almost finished the sketch when her phone rang. John's name came up, instantly killing any sense of joy.

Although he'd kept calling her, she hadn't talked to him since yesterday when she was in the hotel parking lot. She'd quit answering his texts too.

She sucked in a breath and answered. "Hi."

"Hi?" His voice dripped with resentment. "Hi? That's all you have to say to me? Hi? What the fuck, Kita!" He hardly ever said the f-word. "You left our daughter in jail. I mean you left, just left. You sent me some cryptic text about picking your car up or it would get towed. Where the hell are you? You didn't fly anywhere. I checked our credit cards. Last thing you bought were some groceries from Hy-Vee. Where the hell are you?"

"I'm fine. I'm with friends. Is Georgia home? Is she okay?"

"No, she's not okay. Her mother left her in jail. The charges are ridiculous anyway. I'm getting them dropped, but you need to come home. She needs you. I don't have time—"

"Well, you'll have to make time because I'm not coming back. Not right now. Once I know what I'm doing, I'll let you know. Right now I just need time."

"And what are you going to do for money?" he seethed. "Because I can change our credit cards, take your name off the bank accounts. And then what will you do?"

Talking to him, listening to him exhausted her. He was even more exhausting than Georgia was. "I'll survive, that's what I'll do. Bye, John." She turned her phone off and felt some of the exhaustion lift.

She grabbed her sketchbook and pencils again and sketched Ripple and Sonny lounging on the bed at the back of the bus, needing to immerse herself in the sketch, in the nuances and shadows and lines and magic that emerged from her pencils.

She wasn't the artist she once was, the one who had a scholarship to college, but the artist was still there, fighting to come through.

##

Saturday, June 27: Evanston, Wyoming

They pulled into the campground around 6:00 that evening. Nate said they weren't in any hurry. They were picking up a few people in Utah tomorrow, which wasn't a far drive, so there was no rush to get there. Kita offered to pay for a camping spot so she could at least get a shower at some point.

She paid with the bank card she'd kept to herself for so many years. The college account her grandma had started for her in sixth grade after one of Kita's sketches garnered state recognition. Then Gram died and Kita got pregnant, and there was no art school. But there was still an account. An account Kita held onto and never let John know about. There wasn't a lot in there, but there was enough for now.

Kita grabbed some wood for a campfire and a few overpriced groceries for supper from the campground's general store.

"You didn't have to pay for all of that," Nate said when she climbed onto the bus, toting the grocery bag and small bundle of wood.

Ripple ran to the front of the bus like Kita had just brought a sack full of Christmas presents. Ripple peeked into the bag.

30

"Oh my god! Smores? Really? I haven't had smores since…" She looked over her shoulder at Sonny who shrugged. "Wait, I don't think I've ever had smores."

Ripple ended up eating only smores for supper that night, savoring every bite. Her face was dotted with sticky marshmallow pieces and smears of melted chocolate. When she finished her last one, she grabbed Sonny's hand. "Come on," she said, pulling him toward the bus.

A few moments later, laughter and giggling escaped through the partially opened window in the back of the bus. The giggles morphed into moans of pleasure, making Kita blush. She glanced at Nate, who sat on the ground near the fire pit. At least it was dark, hiding her red cheeks. The only light came from the soft glow of the coals in the fire pit.

Nate acted like he didn't hear anything coming from the back of the bus. He reached into his jacket pocket and pulled out a half smoked joint and a lighter. He lit it and inhaled, long and deep. Then he held the joint out toward her. "Want some?"

The complete insanity of the last twenty-four hours flashed through her mind. Why not do one more crazy thing? Besides, she'd smoked pot a couple of times in high school. She sat beside Nate and took the glowing joint from his hand. His fingers brushed hers and he paused to look at her. There seemed to be questions in his eyes, in his fingertips, questions that made her skin tingle, that made her want to get closer. Then his touch was gone and the questions dissipated into the night air, unanswered.

Kita took the joint and inhaled, just a little, just to see how strong it was.

They passed it back and forth in silence, Kita inhaling a little deeper each time. Each inhale settled her a little more, a little deeper into the ground until it felt like she had roots connecting her to the earth. Her limbs relaxed and she let out an audible breath. "God that feels good," she said.

"It does."

"I didn't remember what it felt like to just relax. To just be. To not worry about anyone or anything. God, that feels good."

Nate scooted a little closer then grinned at her, the light from the coals glowing in his eyes. "Are you glad you came?" His pupils became the warm embers.

"Yeah." There were a thousand feelings, a thousand longings, a thousand dreams wrapped up in that one word.

"I didn't think you would."

"Me neither."

He looked at her, really looked at her, then glanced at the ground. "But you left people behind. People who miss you."

He must have overheard her conversation with John. It took her a moment to answer. "Miss me? No. I think me being gone is just inconvenient for them, so no, they don't miss me."

"And, um, do you miss them?" The question was back in his eyes along with something else. Vulnerability?

She shook her head. She didn't miss John. Hadn't missed him for a long, long time. Not since his second affair when Georgia was seven. "I miss my daughter. I miss the person who's in there somewhere. She's just really lost."

"Like you?" His voice was soft like the night air.

She'd never seen it before, never seen that Georgia was just as lost as she was. Just as sad.

She swallowed against the knot in her throat and nodded. "And what about you? she asked, trying to look deeper into his eyes, his face.

"I'm trying to find my way."

Her smile was almost involuntary. "On the Freedom Road?" she asked.

He chuckled and returned the smile.

"How long have you had your bus?"

"It's not really mine. It's my best friend, Blake's." He swallowed like he had his own lump in his throat. "I mean, it was Blake's."

He didn't have to say any more about Blake. "How long has he been gone?"

Nate looked down and drew patterns in the dirt with his finger. "Three years now."

She remembered what Nate had said that morning about being halfway up the mountain, terrified to go forward, but unable to turn back. "Was he the one who left you halfway up the mountain?"

"No. He was already at the top. He knew…he knew about life, about what was important. He kept telling me that I could go to college when I was fifty, but then I had my parents in my head, messing with it, telling me I'd already climbed mountains every summer, that I couldn't throw away the scholarship I'd gotten just to climb a few more."

"Wait," she said, holding up her hand. "Climbing mountains was real? I thought it was just a metaphor you used this morning when you were talking to me. Some metaphor about life."

He laughed, the first full, real laugh she'd heard from him. He laughed until it seemed to envelope the sky. She laughed too, although hers didn't reach as far.

"They were real," he finally said after his laughter faded. "Every summer Blake and I climbed every mountain we could in Colorado. Then we branched out to Utah and New Mexico. Then we got a map of the US." Nate let out a long sigh, a sigh that settled him back into the earth next to her. "Blake bought this bus and took the map. I took college. I guess I fell off the mountain first."

His last words made her shiver. "He fell?" She wondered if she'd overstepped some bounds by asking. "He fell off a mountain?"

Nate leaned forward and rubbed his face with his hands. "Yeah, and I should have been there. I should have been with him. Then maybe he'd be…"

She wanted to move closer, to put her arm around him, comfort him. She just wanted to be closer, to feel his hand on hers, to touch his face, to feel the contrast of his scratchy stubble with the smoothness of his cheekbones. She wanted to know what his lips would feel like on hers, what his hands would feel like on her skin. She wanted to say his name so he'd know, so he'd hear it in her voice.

She was about to say his name when Ripple opened the bus door and hopped down the steps. "I could really use a shower," she exclaimed to the world. She looked at Kita. "You want to come with me?"

Kita didn't want to go. She wanted to stay with Nate, but Nate had already stood up and was poking at the coals with a stick.

It was late when Kita and Ripple walked to the shower. The winding roads through the campground were silent.

Kita was quiet, preoccupied while she undressed in the shower stall and washed herself in the slow stream of water. What she'd felt when she was with Nate caught her by surprise. Those feelings, that heat in her stomach, that pull toward another person was foreign after so many years of a dead marriage.

"Shit," Ripple's voice came from the next stall. "Can you come help me? My bra's stuck in my hair."

"Just a minute," Kita called back as she finished pulling her clothes on.

Kita wasn't sure how it happened, but the clasps on Ripple's bra had somehow gotten caught in the back of her wet dreadlocks. When Kita went to try to free the bra, she sucked in a breath and took a few steps back. Ripple's back was covered in old scars. Most were white. A few that looked like burn marks had a pinkish tint.

She couldn't hide the look of horror from Ripple. "I'm sorry," Kita said, "I just didn't expect…" She moved closer again and freed the bra from Ripple's wet hair, then clasped it for her, wishing she could think of something to say.

"My mom used to think I was trying to steal her boyfriends," Ripple said. "It made her do some crazy things, especially when she was using." Ripple wrapped her arms around herself as if to shield herself. "Funny thing is that those guys hit on me instead of the other way around."

"I'm so sorry." It was the only thing she could think of to say.

Ripple slipped into some old leggings and an oversized sweater. "You know, I forget about those scars sometimes now. Now that I'm in this life with Sonny. When I meet people like you and Nate, I forget. Mostly."

Kita wanted to know more about the scars, but it felt too intrusive to ask. "How long have you known Sonny?"

"We met at a gathering two years ago. I was traveling with a few other people I met on the road. They were headed to the Rainbow Gathering, and I wanted to check it out. Sonny and some of his friends had an old van back then. We were flying a sign and he picked us up. I wasn't looking for anyone. Didn't want to hook up with anyone. But me and Sonny…we were supposed to find each other."

"Is your real name Ripple?"

She was quiet for a moment, her eyes looking pained as they stared past Kita. "It is now. Sonny's the one who first called me Ripple, you know, cuz of the Grateful Dead song. He says I'm a ripple, even when the water is still and silent."

"He's right," Kita said. "And was Sonny always Sonny?"

Ripple giggled. "Yeah, from the day he was born. Did you know he was born at a Rainbow Gathering?"

"Really?"

"Yeah, I think it's why he's so…well, so Sonny. He's good and wonderful." Ripple looked at Kita like she was seeing through her battered spirit. "Kind of like you."

Kita's heart swelled like it used to with Georgia, before Georgia hated her. It seemed unfathomable that Ripple's mother could ever be cruel to such a beautiful soul.

"I hope—" Kita swallowed against the emotion rising in her throat. "I hope you know how beautiful you are. How strong you are. I can't imagine the courage it took for you to leave when you were just—how old were you?"

"It was three years ago, so I was fifteen."

"Fifteen?" Kita shook her head, feeling ashamed. "I wish I had half the courage you have." Ripple's hell made Kita's hell look like heaven. "I've been a coward all these years, feeling sorry for myself because my husband didn't love me, and somewhere along the way my daughter went from being my best friend to hating me. And I just sat there for years, like there was no other choice."

Ripple took Kita's hand and led her to the bench in the bathroom. "But you're not sitting there anymore. You're with us."

"And I'm scared to death. I don't know what I'm doing, Ripple. I don't know how you did it. How did you do it?"

Ripple squeezed her hand. "Shit, I didn't know what I was doing when I left either. You don't think I was terrified? Not everyone you meet on the road is like Sonny or Nate."

"I'm glad you found them."

A shadow passed over Ripple's normally bright green eyes. "Me too. And I'm glad you found us."

Everything in Kita's chest expanded, making it hard to breathe. "I should have done this sooner." She gripped Ripple's hand like it was a lifeline. "Why didn't I see I had a choice? I wasted so much time. So much time."

"But you still got a lot of time left too," Ripple said, with the kind of wisdom no eighteen-year-old should have. "I mean, how old are you?"

"Thirty-six."

"You probably have more than half your life left. That's good. Even if you only had a year left, at least you have a year. Or even a month." Ripple grinned like she'd discovered the secret of life. "Man, you got on the right bus at the right time."

Something about the way Ripple said it made Kita laugh. She laughed so hard, the swelling in her chest dissipated. The weight on her heart and lungs was expelled with each exhale of pure laughter. Ripple laughed with her, that beautiful, musical laugh that was in harmony with Kita's. Laughter that sounded like heaven.

Kita wiped the tears that had poured out with her laughter. "I think I did get on the right bus." Kita grabbed her towel and ran it over her hair one last time. "We should probably get back to that bus."

They walked hand in hand down the dimly lit path back to Nate's bus. Right before Kita was about to knock on the bus door, Ripple stopped her. "Your daughter is real lucky to have a mom like you."

Kita shook her head. "She doesn't think so."

"Someday she'll see it," Ripple said with a certainty that Kita lacked.

##

Sunday, June 28: Heber Valley, Utah

The stars looked so bright against the ebony canopy of sky, they didn't seem real. Millions or billions stared down at Kita at the campground outside of Heber Valley. They weren't far from the sight of the Rainbow Gathering, but they'd gotten into Heber Valley late enough, they decided to wait until morning to make the final, short leg of the drive.

Their camping spot was louder, livelier than it was the night before. In total, they'd picked up eight more people. Most of them were young, like Sonny and Ripple. There was an older guy, Coyote Joe, who'd been going to gatherings since the early 1980's. Kita listened to his stories while she sketched him and others on the bus.

She leaned against the bus and looked at the circle of people around the campfire. Two guys played guitar while a girl joined in on the banjo. Coyote Joe lit a small pipe and passed it around.

Kita looked for Nate but didn't see him. He'd taken some of his stuff from the bus about an hour ago and disappeared. She hadn't had much of a chance to talk to him since last night. He seemed to be in his own world while he was driving, but whenever they stopped somewhere, he'd give her a glance or a smile. It made her wonder if he'd felt anything last night.

She was about to go sit beside Coyote Joe when Nate's silhouette materialized from some trees as he walked toward the bus. He gave everyone around the fire a nod, but walked straight toward Kita.

When he reached her, he gave her one of his rare smiles. He held out a joint, this time a whole one. "You want to go share it?" he asked, nodding in the direction of the trees.

"Yeah." She wanted to share a lot more than the joint.

"Hold on," he said, then ran onto the bus. A few moments later, he came out with a thick jacket. "I think I'll need this."

Nate had told her how cold it would be, especially at the gathering where the elevation was over 10,000 feet. They'd stopped at a camping supply outlet earlier in the day and Nate had helped her pick out a good sleeping bag, tent, and some warm clothes. She also bought good wool hats and gloves for Sonny and Ripple.

Kita followed Nate through a small grove of trees to what looked like the far edge of the campground. There were no other tents or RVs in sight. Nate had set up his tent in a small clearing there. His sleeping bag sat on the ground outside of his tent.

"C'mon." He grabbed her hand and walked toward the sleeping bag. How long had it been since she'd held someone's hand? A man's hand. By the time Georgia had outgrown holding Kita's hand, so had John.

They sat across from each other on the sleeping bag and Nate lit the joint. This time Kita didn't hesitate when she inhaled. By the time they were halfway through the joint, Kita was somehow rooted to the earth and pulled to the sky at the same time. She used to be tiny, invisible. But now she existed, now she sprouted from the earth toward the sky, taking up space.

Nate turned toward her. "Why'd you come? Why'd you get on the bus?" He shifted his weight, looking nervous.

She could have written a book in response to his question, but she was worried if he knew who she was before, he'd find an excuse to leave the space they were in. "I told you…I just couldn't go home."

"Why?"

Kita shook her head. "If you knew, you'd think—you'd…" The words were stuck in her chest. It was like she could see the letters, the words that were lodged there, waiting for her to breathe them where the night air would sweep them away.

He reached out and put his hand on her knee, but just for the span of several beats. It was gone too soon. "You don't know what I'll think, just like I didn't know what you'd think when I told you about Blake and how I didn't have the guts to go with him." He plucked a piece of grass and shredded it. "I don't think you're that different than me. I think you wished you would have left sooner, too."

The statement was like steel in her gut. "I should have, but I was too scared. Now I wonder if I had left when Georgia was little, maybe things would be different with her. Better."

"So you're, uh, you're married," he stammered.

"No." The word was carried out on the frost of her breath. It was like setting the truth free. "There's a piece of paper, but that's all that's left of my marriage. I don't say a word about his lovers and he pretty much leaves me alone." She reached for the joint that dangled from Nate's thumb and forefinger. The last thing she wanted to talk about was John, but she did. The story spilled out on frosty streams of breath and smoke about how she got pregnant right after her grandma died, how she had Georgia at seventeen, how she never even got to look at a mountain, let alone climb it.

She looked at Nate, wondering if her tangled words had made sense. Somehow even in the darkness, she saw his face, his eyes. His eyes were a shiny sapphire that deepened to the darkest shade of blue, the night sky. Stars swam in his irises, dipping in and out of sight like falling stars. Like shooting stars.

Make a wish, Kita dear, Gram's voice whispered through the trees, their arms reaching for her like Gram's, protecting her.

What should I wish for?

It's your wish, sweetie. Just make it a good one.

"I wish you were here," she whispered to the shooting stars in Nate's eyes.

"I'm right here." The words fell out of Nate's mouth like water. Gram's voice was gone, leaving her there with Nate and the billions of stars cascading around them.

She moved closer to Nate, no longer afraid to reach for his hand. He laced his fingers with hers and lifted them to his mouth to kiss them. Warmth spread from her knuckles like soft hues of orange and gold through her veins, exploding when it reached her heart.

Nate leaned forward and kissed her, soft, tentative. Years of dormant need, want, desire pulsed through her, stronger with each kiss until her veins burned red. She lay back on the sleeping bag and pulled Nate with her. The steam from their breath collided in the air, fusing together.

"You want to go in the tent?" Nate asked.

"No." She didn't want to leave the clearing or the stars or the trees.

Nate stretched and reached inside the tent and pulled out a thick blanket. "So we don't freeze."

They shed their coats and pulled the blanket over them. Kita kissed Nate again, no longer soft, tentative kisses. She pressed herself against him and his whole body sighed. When she felt his hand beneath her shirt on her ribcage, she shivered. It was a shiver that shed the remnants of who she was. Not the core of who she was, but the calloused skin that covered her core, that buried it. She opened her eyes to the night sky and she was Kita again.

Nate must have misjudged the pause she took when she opened her eyes. "Are you sure?" he asked. "We don't have to, if you don't—"

"I'm sure." She hoped he heard the truth in her voice. "I haven't wanted this for a long time. Years."

He didn't answer right away, just rubbed the small of her back. "Me neither," he finally said.

"Really?" That shocked her more than anything else he'd told her. She'd made assumptions based on his lifestyle.

"After Blake died…well, I felt dead for a long time. Still do sometimes."

She'd never considered that he might not want to sleep with her yet. "We don't have to if you don't—"

She was close enough to see the flecks of light reflected in his sapphire eyes. "I've wanted to since yesterday morning in the rain."

"Me too," she whispered, thinking that yesterday was a lifetime ago.

He kissed her again and slid her shirt off. Needing to feel his skin against hers, she pulled his shirt over his head and ran her hands over his chest. This time he was the one who shivered, who took a deep breath, who gathered her in his arms.

Everything about him, about the moment was beautiful as they shed the rest of their clothes and joined their bodies. They moved to the cadence of the wind, the rustle of the tree branches, the music of their breath, the drum of her pulse in her ears, until it culminated in a swirl of light, like the Milky Way above them.

##

Monday, June 29: Heber Valley, Utah

Kita woke as the sun's soft orange glow pushed away the last traces of night. The sun hadn't yet reached the clearing, and she moved closer to Nate, seeking the warmth of his body. Seeking him.

He stirred and draped his arm across her, pulling her close, letting out a sleepy "Hmmm."

She looked at his face—a mixture of peace lined with traces of pain, the remnants of his own battles. His own struggles to be free. When he opened his eyes and smiled at her, the pain was momentarily erased. "I'm glad you're here," he said.

Her heart thumped so loud, the musical beat traveled from her heart to her head. "Me too."

"You, um, you want to hang out together at the gathering? We could camp together. If you want to. I mean, you're free to go your own way, do your own thing. I just thought…"

She didn't expect the uncertainty in his voice. "Is that what you call this?" she teased. "Hanging out?"

"No, I mean…I just, I wanted to…" Nate shook his head, looking embarrassed. "I don't want to say goodbye."

"Me neither."

He kissed her, a kiss that held the certainty his voice had lacked.

They made love again as the sun hit the treetops and swathed the clearing in sweet, golden light.

She lay close to Nate afterward, her skin damp with sweat despite the morning chill. She took in a deep breath of the crystalline air and wondered how many more mornings there would be like this. "Where will you go after the gathering?" she asked.

"Probably California. There's usually a regional gathering there a little while after the big Annual Gathering. Then, I don't know. I thought about going up to Mount Shasta, stay there a little while, work a little. It was one of Blake's favorite places." Nate raised himself up on his elbow. "You never made it to Mt. Shasta?"

Kita thought about the trip she'd planned so many years ago. "No."

"You wanna go with me after the gathering?" This time his voice didn't waver.

"I'd like that." By then she might be ready to talk to Georgia. Hopefully Georgia would be ready to talk to her too. Really talk. The time apart might help them broach the chasm between them.

The sound of Ripple calling Kita's name pulled her from her thoughts.

Kita grabbed her clothes. "I should see what she wants."

"She probably wants to make sure you didn't run off." Nate pulled his clothes on, too.

Kita walked hand in hand with Nate back to the bus. When they neared the bus, the smell of coffee wafted toward them. Sonny and Ripple already had a fire going. Coyote Joe plucked a song on his mandolin.

The sight of them filled her heart.

HOBO'S LULLABY

Wednesday, June 24

Thank god there were only fifteen more miles to Boulder. The twelve-hour drive had taken a toll on Maddy and her old car. She'd just filled up with gas, grabbed a bottle of water and some sad looking convenience store fruit, and was ready to make the last leg of today's drive.

She patted the dashboard. "I know you're weary, but we're almost there." The two thousand plus mile journey she'd taken so far hadn't been easy on her little 1986 Suzuki Samurai. She started the engine and put it in reverse. The clutch didn't engage. Nothing happened.

"Dammit," she sighed, her shoulders slumping. She'd been nursing the clutch for a while now, but thought she'd have more time. She at least thought she'd make it to the Rainbow Gathering next week. Boulder was meant to be a place to stop and rest, play a few gigs to make some money before she headed to Utah for the gathering.

She popped the hood and walked around to look beneath it. Although she had a basic working knowledge of how to change filters and sparkplugs and oil, she didn't have a clue how to fix her clutch. It was probably pointless to look under the hood, but maybe by some miracle, she'd find a loose or broken belt, something that could easily be replaced.

"You need some help?"

The voice behind her made her jump and smack her head against the hood. "Fuck!" she growled, then turned to face the idiot.

He was a tall blond guy around her age—late twenties, maybe thirty. "Sorry, I'm really sorry. You okay?"

"You shouldn't sneak up on people," she grumbled, massaging her scalp. There was already a bump there.

"I just wanted to see if you needed help."

"Can you fix a broken clutch?" She didn't mean to sound so rude, but any hint of the good mood she'd had a few minutes ago was ruined.

He walked up to the car and bent over the engine. "Are you sure that's what's wrong?"

"I'm not an idiot. I do know a thing or two about cars."

He held his hands up and took a step back. "I didn't mean…" He sighed and shoved his hands in the pockets of his dark brown hiking shorts. "I guess I've completely screwed up any chance of making a good first impression."

She gave him a half smile. "Pretty much."

"I really was just seeing if you needed help."

Maddy shut the hood and leaned back against the green mini SUV. She'd gotten it while she was still in med school and had gotten especially attached to it after hitting the road. "I think he's going to need more help than I can give him," she sighed.

He crinkled his forehead. "Him?"

"Yeah, my car. It's just a habit. He's been my only traveling companion for the last six months or so." She looked at the only other car at the convenience store, which was parked by the gas tanks. The old Toyota had Colorado plates. "Are you from around here?"

He nodded. "I live in Boulder."

"You wouldn't happen to know of a good garage or mechanic who won't charge me too much, would you?"

"Actually, yeah. My cousin works at a little place run by an old mechanic. He's helped me keep my bucket of rust going." He nodded at his car. "He might not have all the latest equipment, but Bernie's an honest guy. I can give him a call after I go in and pay for my gas."

Some of the weight lifted from her shoulders and she felt bad for being so gruff at first. "Thanks, that would be great."

When he walked inside to pay, she squinted to take a better look at his rusted car and the bumper stickers. One was a quote from a Grateful Dead song: *What a long strange trip it's been.* The other one was a little harder to make out. She could read the word in all caps: MUSICIAN. She took a few steps closer to read the smaller words underneath: *Driver Has No Cash.* It made her chuckle out loud. There was no truer statement.

The sound of the door opening behind her made her turn around. She wondered if he'd seen her staring at his car. If he had, he didn't say anything about it. He walked over to her and pulled out his phone. She listened while he talked to someone about towing her car.

When he got off the phone, she couldn't read his expression. "Someone can come and get it, but not until at least seven or eight tonight. Bernie won't be able to look at it until tomorrow."

The relief she'd felt earlier was short lived. "Dammit. Only fifteen more miles, that's all I wanted for now."

"Are you headed to Boulder?"

"Yeah, just for the week."

He rocked back on his heels and looked at her car. "I could give you a ride if you need one, at least to the garage so you can talk to Bernie and give him your keys."

She shouldn't. All the rules of the world and all the rules of the road screamed against taking rides with people you didn't know, especially if you were a woman. It would be a stupid thing to do, like playing Russian Roulette. A wave of nausea coursed through her. She'd already faced worse odds than that, had lost, and still came out on the other side of it.

Taking a ride from this guy probably wasn't any riskier than the nights she'd slept in her car at rest stops along the interstate. He hadn't given her any weird vibes yet, and she'd learned to trust her gut.

"I don't know, I should probably wait with my car." She wanted to see how he'd react if she turned him down. If he was persistent, she'd walk away and find her own tow truck.

"Fair enough," he said. "Best of luck to you. I hope Bernie can get your friend up and running again."

"Me too. Thanks for your help."

He was halfway to his car when she called out to him. "Hey."

He turned around.

"Are you really a musician?" she asked.

He looked confused. "Yeah, why?"

"I'll take that ride if the offer still stands."

He smiled at her. "I'll bring my car over."

Thankfully she packed light. A camping backpack held her tent, sleeping bag, a warm coat, and a few changes of clothes, along with some nonperishable food. A smaller bag held her personal items. The last thing was her acoustic guitar.

When she leaned in to throw the fruit and water into her bag, her long blonde hair fell out of the quick, messy bun she'd done at 4:00 a.m. She quickly pulled it back again, not bothering to look at it in the car mirror. It didn't matter. She wasn't trying to win any beauty contests or pick up any guys.

The guy opened the trunk for her where she deposited her backpack. She slid her guitar into the back seat, then ran back to her car. "Bye, Woody," she whispered and patted the hood. "See you tomorrow."

She turned to see the guy looking at her, his eyebrows raised in amusement. "What was that about?"

"Nothing," she said, putting her chin in the air as she walked around to the passenger door of his car.

"I'm Duncan, by the way," he said after they'd both gotten in.

"Maddy." She held out her hand.

His grip was strong, and his calloused fingertips told her he was probably a guitar or bass player.

"Are *you* a musician?" he asked as he pulled away from the gas station.

"I play a little guitar, sing some, write some songs every once in a while."

"Is that a yes?"

She shrugged. "I like singer songwriter better. I know it's not true, but musician makes me think of someone who plays in the symphony. Or some band who plays in cheap hotel lounges.

"Thanks," he said sarcastically.

"I didn't mean you." She gave him an evil grin. "Unless you play in cheap hotel lounges."

"I play wherever I can get paid." She couldn't tell by his tone if he was put off by what she'd said.

She looked at his profile, thinking that with his sun-kissed hair and tall build, he'd fit right in on the beaches of California. At least she thought he might. She hadn't made it to California yet. "Do you play electric or acoustic or bass?" she asked.

"Acoustic mostly. Sometimes when I get together with my roommate and our friends, I'll play an electric guitar, but it's really not my thing." He looked at her and smiled. "No, we're not a band, and no, we don't play the hotel circuit."

It was a twenty-mile drive to Bernie's Auto Shop. They talked about music for the rest of the drive, their conversation melting away the miles. She was a little sad when he pulled up to the auto shop. It had been that way with other people she'd met during her journey. The people who crossed her path for a few days or a few hours or a few minutes. She wrote about all of them so she wouldn't forget. Or if she did forget, someone could read it to her so she could remember. She'd write about Duncan too.

He turned to face her. "Can I give you my number? Just in case you need something while you're in town."

"Okay." She didn't plan to contact him. It wasn't a good idea to get attached.

She handed him her phone and he typed in his name and number. She didn't offer to give him hers, and he didn't ask.

"Thanks a lot, Duncan, for everything. It was great meeting you."

He leaned forward like he wanted to shake her hand or give her a hug, but he didn't. "You too. Good luck with everything."

##

It was 6:00 p.m. by the time Maddy made it to the Pearl Street Mall in Boulder. She'd heard about the pedestrian mall where street performers, artists, and musicians performed. It sounded like people could make decent money depending on how busy the mall was.

She'd caught a bus near Bernie's that took her to the mall. The sound of music hit her as soon as her feet touched the cobblestone street. Up ahead, four drummers pounded out a rhythm that pulsed through the air. They were so engrossed in the beat and the harmony of the drums, they barely seemed to notice the people watching them. Farther down there was a juggler and an acrobat. It made Maddy want to walk the length of the mall to take in the sights and the other performers, but she was so tired, she needed to sit.

She found a quiet spot near a pizza place and pulled out her guitar. When she went to play a few warm-up scales and chords, her right hand jerked, hitting the strings, making a jangling noise.

"Shit," she whispered, massaging her hand. It was always worse when she was exhausted or stressed. She leaned back and closed her eyes, taking deep breaths, grounding herself, practicing the meditation techniques she hadn't mastered yet.

After ten minutes, she was ready to play again. This time her body cooperated, and she settled into her usual set of cover songs with a few originals sprinkled in.

By eight o'clock, she'd made enough money to get something to eat, even find a cheap hotel. But if what Bernie had told her about her car was true, she couldn't waste a penny at a restaurant or a hotel, no matter how cheap. If it really was her clutch, it was going to take almost all her reserves to pay for it. To top it off, it would probably be at least a week before he got the parts. He'd said she could go to another mechanic, but they'd all have the same problem getting the parts she needed because it had been years since her car had been manufactured in the US.

The worst part wasn't the money. That was bad, but she could manage. The worst part was the Rainbow Gathering. She'd wanted to go since she'd met a young couple in Nashville a few months ago who told her they were going to the gathering. She'd never heard of a Rainbow Gathering before, but the way Sonny and Ripple talked about it made her want to go. Although they told her it was an annual event, Maddy didn't know if she'd get another chance to go to one.

Right now she needed to focus on what to do tonight. She'd find a grocery store to get a few staples and hopefully find a safe place to sleep. Normally, she would have camped somewhere, but the nearest camping spots were miles outside of Boulder, so she had no way of getting to any of those. It looked like there were some people hanging out at the Pearl Street Mall who didn't have beds or homes. Some held signs asking for money for food. She could ask around and find out where they slept.

She put her guitar in its case and stood up. Although performing could be tiring, it mentally energized her, especially when people stopped to listen like they did tonight. She had enough adrenaline to hoist her backpack to her shoulders and walk down the length of the mall.

The sun had given way to dusk, and the mall was lit with a warm orange glow from the shop windows and streetlights. An acrobat performed for a growing crowd. Maddy stopped to watch for a few minutes, amazed by the woman's talent.

A cellist played a few yards away from the acrobat. The sound was so sweet and rich, Maddy swore she saw the notes crescendo until they reached the treetops and floated away in the twilight. She'd seen her share of incredible street musicians, especially in Nashville. The talent in Boulder was some of the best she'd heard so far.

She was about two thirds of the way down the street when a voice and guitar caught her attention. There were technically great singers, and then there were the singers who pulled you in with their emotion, their depth. She'd take depth over technique any day. This guy had a good voice, not perfect, but good, but that's not what called her to him. The way he sang the words to his acoustic version of Mumford and Sons' "I Will Wait" made her think he'd lived every word.

He was kitty corner on the other side of the street, and she cut across to get a closer listen. It was hard to make him out since he sat in the shadows. Although a few people gathered around him to listen, he seemed to be in his own world where only he and the music existed. When she was just a few yards away, she stopped as soon as she recognized him. Although Duncan claimed to be a musician, she honestly hadn't thought he'd be this good. She thought he might be a pretty boy who played to get the attention of women. She'd couldn't have been more wrong.

She stood back until the song was over. A few people dropped some money in his guitar case and walked away.

"Not bad for a musician," she said as she walked up to him.

He gave her a smart-ass grin. "Thanks, I think."

"You were really good, I mean it."

"You sound surprised."

She sat beside him on the bench. "A little."

He glanced at her guitar case. "Did you play?"

"Yeah, up at the other end of the mall. The talent here is amazing."

"It is." He looked at her backpack that she'd set on the ground. "Any word from Bernie about your car?"

She filled him in on the bad news.

"Well, if you're going to be stuck somewhere for a little while, Boulder's a good place to be. Especially for a musician."

"I know, it's just… I had someplace I wanted to be next week."

"That sucks."

"Yeah, it does," she sighed. "Well, I should get going and let you get back to playing."

She was about to get up when his voice stopped her. "Do you want to play a few songs together?"

"Really? Right here, without ever practicing together? You don't even know if I'm any good."

He nudged her shoulder. "I'll take my chances. Besides, things are slowing down, so if we really suck, not many people will hear."

She smiled at him. "You're not worried about losing your street credibility?"

He laughed at her comment. "I don't think I had much to begin with. Come on, it'll be fun. I know about every acoustic cover under the sun."

"Me too. What do you want to play?"

He leaned back and looked at the light blanket of stars that were just starting to sprinkle the hazy purple sky. "How about a real duet? I don't get to do those often. You know the acoustic duet to Time After Time?"

"I love that song." It was one she'd played quite a bit, minus the duet part.

She pulled out her guitar and they decided which key to sing it in. Maddy never had much of a chance to play or sing with anyone else, except her dad. He'd taught her to play when she was a kid. From the time she learned her first song, she was addicted, and played constantly until she went to college. Then med school, her internship, and her first year of residency took over her life, leaving her music and her guitar in a dusty corner. She'd only picked it up again after leaving her residency and her life out east behind. Music had reconnected her to herself in a way nothing else did. This was the first time she was sharing it with someone else since she'd started her trip.

Playing with Duncan wasn't what she expected. She was nervous when they first started, nervous she'd mess up, but after they made it through the intro, she settled into the music, immersing herself in the emotion, the meaning of the lyrics. They kept their eyes locked while they sang, silently communicating with a nod or a look so they could stay in sync. By the time she harmonized on the chorus with him, she was lost in the song, lost in the way their voices melded together, lost in what felt like magic.

When they finished, the sound of applause brought her back to the real world, if you could call the Pearl Street Mall the real world.

Duncan didn't take his eyes off her even when someone put a few dollars in his guitar case. "So," he finally said, leaning on his guitar, "that was…you're…you're really something."

She wrinkled her forehead. "I'm not sure that's a compliment."

"Trust me, it is."

She was glad the darkness hid the flush in her cheeks.

"Do you have time to play a few more?" Duncan asked.

Energy surged through her, making her feel like she could play for hours. "I don't have anywhere else to be."

They played for another hour. By that time, her hands were fatigued and she didn't want to risk having a spasm while she played.

She looked down after they finished their last song, not wanting to look at him, not wanting to say goodbye.

"You want to grab something to eat?" he asked, giving her a hopeful look,

Her stomach growled making her realize how hungry she was. She almost said yes, then remembered she couldn't spend the money and she shouldn't spend any more time with Duncan. She reluctantly shook her head. "Thanks, but I should really go."

"I'll treat," he said. "I made some okay money tonight. There's a great pizza place over there. Probably the best pizza you'll ever eat."

She couldn't help but smile at him. "The best pizza ever is in Boulder? Really? What about Chicago's famous pizza?"

"This beats them all, but you'll never know if you don't try it."

Tell him no. "Well, I guess I have to try it now." She wanted to kick herself.

The pizza was like eating a slice of heaven. The soft crust was topped with veggies and wonderfully gooey, greasy cheese. So much cheese. She rarely allowed herself to eat like that, sticking to the healthiest, cleanest diet possible, even on the road.

Duncan laughed at the face she made when she took her first bite.

"Oh my god," she said, her mouth full of pizza. "I think I'm gonna have a foodgasm."

He laughed even harder. "I haven't heard that term before."

"Seriously, this is the best thing I've had in months. The road doesn't always lend itself to good food."

"Where are you headed?" he asked. "I mean once your car is fixed."

She wasn't about to go into the reason for her journey, but she could talk around it. "A little bit of everywhere, I guess. But I was planning to check out the Rainbow Gathering in Utah. It starts next week, but now, without my car, I don't know."

He took a drink of his beer. "I've heard a few people around here talk about it. There was a sign up at one of the health food stores—someone looking for a ride there. I don't know much about it though."

She put down her second piece of pizza, which was almost gone. "Me neither, but I wanted to check it out. It sounds like something everyone should do at least once in their life. I met a really cool couple in Nashville who were going. It's a weeklong thing where a bunch of people gather in a national forest and create this whole community. Kind of a throwback to the hippie days. Peace, love, family. And music…lots of music."

He chuckled. "You sure you're not being lured into some cult?"

She took a drink of her water, wishing it was beer. "I don't think so. I looked it up online. They've been having gatherings every year since the 70s. I've seen a few videos and even some documentaries. It looks pretty amazing."

He cocked his head at her, looking intrigued. "And then?"

"And then what?"

"And then where are you headed, after your gathering?"

"Did anyone ever tell you that you ask a lot of questions?"

"Sorry," he said, leaning back in his chair, looking a little embarrassed. "Is that your way of telling me to mind my own business?"

"Kind of," she said in a quiet voice. The answer to his question would lead him to ask her why she was traveling around the country and she wasn't ready to tell him. No one but she and her mom knew. And Keith.

"Fair enough," he said.

They finished off the pizza, the conversation turning back to the safer topic of music. She put down a half-eaten piece of pizza and put her hand on her stomach. "That really was the best pizza ever. Thanks," she said, hoping he knew how grateful she was for everything—for the chance to share music, for the good conversation and food. Now she needed to leave. "Tonight was…it was really great."

He leaned forward and looked at her, his blue eyes catching the light from the lamp above their table. "It was."

She sighed and pushed her chair back.

"You don't have anywhere to stay, do you," he said. It wasn't a question.

"I'll find someplace. I'm pretty resourceful."

"I can see that."

She stretched and reached for her bag.

"You can crash at my place if you want to," he said. "No pressure, no strings. You can crash on my couch. My roomate's up in Estes Park for a few days, playing some gigs there, so it's just me at the apartment. It's better than sleeping out in the cold."

It was late and she was beyond tired. He hadn't tried anything with her, hadn't given her any indication that he expected or even wanted her to sleep with him. "You mean it?" she asked, feeling emotional for some reason. "I can sleep on your couch and you won't—"

"I won't," he finished.

Duncan's apartment wasn't far from the University of Colorado campus. It took him less than five minutes to show her his tiny apartment, which consisted of two small bedrooms, a barren living room and kitchenette.

"Sorry," he said as he set her backpack down by the threadbare couch. "It's not much to look at."

"Oh, it's the Hilton compared to some of the places I've stayed."

"That's the first and last time I'll ever hear that comparison," he laughed.

"No, it's good," she said. "It's great, actually."

He leaned against the couch. "Make yourself at home. There's not much in the fridge, but help yourself. The bathroom's through there." He pointed down the tiny hallway. "Couch is here. I'll grab you some blankets from my room."

She sat on the couch and absentmindedly poked some loose stuffing back into a cushion while she wondered if it was really the right decision to stay with him. He was back in just a minute with a fleece blanket, a worn comforter, and a pillow.

"Let me know if you need anything else," he said as he set the blankets and pillow beside her. "Well," he rocked back on his heels, his eyes on the ground. "Goodnight."

"Goodnight," she whispered.

She wanted to tell him thanks again and that she'd be out of his hair tomorrow, but he'd already gone to his room.

Maddy tried to settle in. The old couch was surprisingly comfortable, but she was restless. After a half hour, she went to the bathroom and changed into an old t-shirt and athletic shorts, thinking they'd be more comfortable to sleep in.

When she got back to the couch, she pulled the comforter over her and settled her head on the pillow. They smelled like him. Although she hadn't been close enough to really smell him, she was pretty sure that the hint of deodorant mixed with the unmistakable earthy scent of a man belonged to Duncan. The smell made her even more restless because it took her back to the mall, to the way he looked at her when they sang together, the way he laughed when pizza cheese dripped down her chin. The way he told her there were no expectations and no strings, and he meant it.

This was why she didn't do this. Almost everything else on her journey was on the table except for this. No hooking up and no getting involved with anyone. She rolled over to her other side and flopped her head down on the pillow. But why? Why was it off the table? She wanted to live, really live. Wasn't this part of living? She told herself to shut up, to close her eyes and try to meditate.

Time got lost in a series of turning over, sitting up, and flopping back down. The more she silently begged for sleep the more it ran from her. She took in a breath of frustration, forgetting that she'd be inhaling him too. God, that smell, those eyes. It had been so long. Too long.

No.

But he was good, different. She pictured him playing his guitar, his fingers on the strings. The fingers she wanted to feel in her hair, on her skin.

Maddy threw the covers off and got up. "You're an idiot," she hissed at herself as she walked toward Duncan's room.

His door was open. She could barely make out the shape of his body in the darkness. She craned her neck, trying to see if he was asleep, or if he was restless like her. It looked like he might actually be asleep. She lightly knocked on his door frame.

No response. There was still time to go back to the couch.

She knocked louder.

He stirred, then sat up. "Maddy?" he said in a scratchy voice.

"I, um…" She scuffed the bare carpet with her heel. "I don't want to sleep on the couch."

He didn't say anything, just held his hand out to her.

"No strings?" she asked, her voice shaking.

"No strings," he whispered.

She went to him then—with no hesitation—into his bed, into his arms. She straddled him and peeled off her shirt. He sighed and ran his hands up her sides, over her shoulders and to her face, holding it gently. The way he looked at her—with tenderness wrapped around desire—set her body, her heart on fire. She leaned down to kiss him and he pulled her close. She rested her head in the crook of his neck and took in a breath. He smelled even better than she imagined.

She kissed him again, and when they touched each other, when their bodies joined and moved together, it was just like singing with him.

Thursday, June 25

Maddy woke, still in a sleepy haze, feeling warmer than she had since she'd started her journey six months ago. She settled into the warmth, not wanting to open her eyes. It wasn't just the bed and the blankets that surrounded her in a soft cocoon, it was Duncan's arms around her, his chest for a pillow.

Last night came back to her like dreams sometimes did when she first woke. But last night was better than a dream. As much as she wanted to lay there enveloped in the delicious memories, she needed to leave. She'd had her little fantasy and now it was time to get back to the real world. But the real world was a little too cold, so she settled in deeper, putting her arm across Duncan's stomach.

He stirred at her touch and pulled her closer. "Good morning," he said in a scratchy voice.

"Morning."

He kissed the top of her head and seemed content to lay there in silence, holding her.

The silence poked at Maddy, making her wonder what it meant. He seemed relaxed, but she wondered what he was thinking, if it was a mistake, if he wanted her to leave.

Finally, she pulled away and rolled onto her side where she propped herself up on her elbow to look at him. "Is this gonna be awkward?" she asked.

His confused look told her she'd been wrong about his silence. "I hope not," he answered. "I don't feel awkward, do you?"

"No," she sighed, "but…"

"But what?" he asked when she didn't finish her thought.

"Okay, so this is going to sound really cliché, but I don't normally do this."

He gave her a playful grin, making her wonder if he believed her.

"Well, that's not entirely true. I did this a few times when I was younger…and dumber. But that's not what this trip is about."

His fingers went to her tangled hair. "Are you going to tell me about it now? Your trip?"

She sighed and flopped onto her back, letting her head settle into the pillow. He turned on his side and moved closer to her. The warmth from his naked body, his skin against hers, distracted her.

"Don't laugh at me," she said, trying to focus on something other than how good it felt to be near him.

"I'll try not to."

She rolled her eyes at him. "Thanks for the reassurance."

He shook his head at her. "Will you just tell me?"

"Well, ever since I was a little kid, I wanted to be a singer. People thought it was cute when I was little, but you know, you get older and you're supposed to leave those dreams behind for something more realistic, especially when you're smart. So I went to med school and did my internship and started my residency, and then—"

"Wait, you're a doctor? Like a real doctor?"

"Yeah, but I—I—" Her voice caught, making her stop for a moment. She wasn't going to go there with him. "Well, my dad died, and he was really young, and it made me think about things, really think about things."

"I'm so sorry, Maddy." The look of compassion on his face made her eyes well up, but she fought her tears away.

"He was a really great guy, a musician too, so he was one of the few people who kept telling me to live my dream. After he died, I realized how short life can be, so I walked away from my residency and I'm giving myself at least a year to do this, more if I need it. I want to see the country, take my guitar and play in every state in the continental US."

Everything she'd told him was true, minus a few important details and a bit of a fudged timeline.

He ran his fingers down her arm, creating a rush of goosebumps where his fingers had been. "I can't believe you thought I would laugh at that."

Keith's face flashed through her head. "A lot of people thought I was throwing my life away," she said in a soft voice.

He shook his head. "What you're doing—it takes guts. More guts than I have. I feel like I'm just spinning my wheels here, playing gigs whenever I can, but never really getting anywhere."

She rolled onto her side and faced him, their bodies just inches apart, then she traced his jawline with her finger. "Is that what you want to do? Make it as a singer?"

He took her hand in his. "Sometimes I want to do more, find a way to give back to the world. Sometimes I think about finishing college. I started, but I wasn't focused enough. It's still a sore spot with my parents. But I feel like I need to give this a shot while I can. I don't expect to get famous, but I'd love to release a few songs…or a few albums."

"You shouldn't give up," she said. "You're really good."

He shrugged. "I don't know about that, but thanks." He looked at her with a hint of admiration. "I don't know if I could do what you do. Doesn't it get lonely living on the road?"

Most of the time she welcomed the aloneness, even in the moments when she was forced to face herself. "Not really." She grinned at him. "Besides, I have my faithful traveling companion."

He laughed. "Yeah, I forgot about him. Old what's-his-name."

Her cheeks flushed. "How do you know he has a name?"

"I saw you say something to him yesterday before you got in my car."

"I don't know what you're talking about."

He nudged her. "Come on, what's his name? I won't laugh."

"Woody," she said in a quiet voice, her cheeks growing even hotter.

He burst out laughing, laughing so long it irritated her.

"You're an asshole," she grumbled.

He ran a hand over his face like he was trying to force his laughter away. "I'm sorry, it's just, well, that's quite the name."

She rolled her eyes at him. "Get your head out of the gutter. He's named after Woody Guthrie."

He was quiet for a minute.

"You do know who that is, don't you?"

He looked at her like she was crazy. "Only one of the best songwriters and folk singers in history."

Any irritation washed away. "I guess there is some knowledge in that beautiful head of yours." She moved just a little closer, their skin almost touching.

He closed his eyes and let out a sigh, his breath drawing her to him.

She reached out and traced his lips with her finger. "And here I thought you were just a pretty face with a pretty voice. You've actually got some street credibility."

He laughed again, a deep, husky laugh. "Knowing who Woody Guthrie is gives me street cred?"

She nodded, her hand still on his face. "You're talking to an expert. I've been to a lot of streets over these past six months. I know a thing or two."

Any hint of laughter left his face and he looked at her like he did last night when she came into his room. "Yeah, you do." His voice got softer. "I've never met anyone like you."

She wanted to tell him that he didn't know her, and that getting to know her wouldn't be good for either one of them. But those words died before they ever reached her throat. Instead, she pulled him to her, pressing her naked body against his, drowning in something so new, so beautiful.

Monday, June 29

It seemed like she'd been with Duncan for more than five days. It was one of the easiest, most natural things in her life in a long time. Things with Keith hadn't even been this easy. With him there had been some of that early game playing, some of the guessing, the insecurities.

Maybe things felt so real, so easy because she knew she'd be leaving, so there was no need to wonder about the future, no need to play games. All they had was now, and now would end in the next week or two, whenever her car was fixed. She'd been in contact with Bernie who said he should get the parts sometime next week, then it would only be another day or two before he'd have Woodie Guthrie up and running.

Her leaving was the one thing she and Duncan didn't talk about.

These days with him were some of the fullest she'd lived. They went to Chautauqua Park and hiked up into the Flatirons. They went to coffee shops and health food stores and played at the Pearl Street Mall every evening. While he worked his day job at a local guitar shop, she wrote and worked on songs. At night they lay tangled in bed where they made love and talked and laughed. And every night she told herself she should leave the next day.

Last night was the first time either of them mentioned the future. They'd just made love and lay on top of the messy sheets and blankets. He laced his fingers through hers. "I've been thinking…" he said.

"That sounds like too much work." She scooted closer to him, trying to distract him.

He put his arms around her, pulling her closer, his skin still damp. "I'm serious."

She nibbled at his ear. "I don't want to be serious."

He laughed and gave her a gentle shove. "It's nothing earth shattering. I was just thinking that since Woody Guthrie's not gonna be fixed in time for you to get to the Rainbow Gathering, I could drive you. I'd like to check it out, see what it's like."

Her heart jumped, but she tamped it back down. "You don't have to do that."

"What if I want to?"

She rolled onto her back, putting some space between them. "I'm supposed to make this trip by myself."

When he didn't respond, she turned to look at him and couldn't tell if he was hurt or irritated. "I never said I wanted to follow you around the country. I'd like to check out the gathering and you need a ride. It's nothing more than that," he grumbled.

She raised her eyebrows at him. "You just want to give me a ride there? Nothing else?"

He sat up and leaned against the old headboard. "You know, you don't make this easy." It was the first time she'd heard him sound frustrated. "Do you need me to say it again? The whole no strings thing? It's still no strings, Maddy. I like you a lot, but I'm not gonna get in your way and I'm not gonna ask you to change your plans after the gathering is over."

The things he said rang true. They'd both been up front with each other, him even more than her. There was no reason not to believe him. And she couldn't deny that she craved more time with him.

"Sorry," she said. "I guess I'm a little gun shy."

The left side of his mouth curved up just a little. "I kind of figured that out."

She slid her hand down his arm until her fingers met his. "I'll take you up on your offer, but if we get there and you want to hang out with someone else, you can." She grinned at him. "I've heard there are a lot of naked women there. And men too."

He rolled over on top of her and tickled her, her laughter chasing away any leftover tension. "I already know a naked woman. One's enough for me."

She pulled him closer and kissed him, wondering what it would be like if things were different and they could have a future together. Would she ever get tired of being with him like this?

Now, while she woke up beside Duncan this morning, she tried not to think about that. Instead she let herself sit in the moment, soaking in the kind of contentment that had been missing for a long time. She closed her eyes, letting her breath and the moment ground her.

Finally, she rolled over and laid her arm across his chest. "Hey, sleepyhead," she said, shaking his shoulder.

He opened his eyes and stretched, giving her a groggy smile.

"I'm gonna go make us some coffee," she said, "and then we should go through your stuff today, see if you have everything you need for the gathering. It's backwoods, like real backwoods. No outhouses, no showers, no luxuries. And it's gonna be freezing at night, ten thousand feet up in the mountains."

He wrinkled his brow. "What? Do you think I can't handle roughing it a little?" He looked around his bedroom. "Do I look pampered to you?"

She straddled him and pushed his blond hair out of his eyes. "A little, but I think you'll be okay."

He ran his hands up her ribcage and over her breasts. "Besides, I'll have you to keep me warm."

"Uh huh," she said, feeling him grow hard against her. She leaned down and kissed him, telling herself the coffee could wait.

A half hour later, Maddy walked into the kitchen, wearing one of Duncan's T-shirts. She smiled to herself as she ground the coffee and poured it into the coffee maker. She'd just filled the coffee pot at the sink when her hand spasmed. There was no way to hold on to the coffee pot. She helplessly watched it fall to the floor and shatter.

"Maddy?" Duncan called from the bedroom.

She looked at her hand that still spasmed. It didn't usually last this long. She grabbed it with her other hand and massaged it, trying to hide it. "Fuck," she hissed. "Fuck, fuck, fuck."

It only took a few seconds before Duncan was in the kitchen. He looked from her to the shattered glass on the floor. "Are you okay?"

She tried to replace the fear on her face with embarrassment. "Yeah," she said. "I'm really sorry, I'll buy you a new one."

His eyes went to her hands, making her look away from him.

"I don't care about the coffee pot." There was too much concern in his voice. He walked in front of her and took her hands in his. "Maddy, what's wrong?"

She yanked her hands away. "Nothing," she snapped.

He shook his head. "I've seen you do this…rub your hand like there's something wrong with it. And I've seen you stumble, more than once." He let out a sigh. "I've seen you take pills too."

She looked away from him and stared at the broken glass on the floor. It was like looking at her life—splintered and shattered. She thought she'd hidden all of that from him. "Yeah, I'm a little clumsy," she said more defensively than she meant to. "And everybody takes pills once in a while. You take something when you get a headache, don't you?"

He sighed and took a few steps back to lean against the counter. She couldn't stand the way he looked at her with too much worry. "Something's wrong with you, isn't it," he said.

She backed away from him. "What do you mean?" She couldn't do this. It was another rule. She swore she'd never tell anyone she met during her trip. The last thing she wanted was for people to feel sorry for her. She wanted people to get to know her, just her. Not her disease.

At least Duncan knew enough to keep his distance, but he didn't know enough to shut up. "It's why you don't want any strings attached, isn't it."

She shook her head. "I don't—I don't— Just drop it, Duncan. Please."

His eyes pleaded with her. "You can tell me, whatever it is. It'll be okay."

His last statement punched her. It couldn't be further from the truth. "Okay? Okay?! It will never be okay!"

He winced at her onslaught, but his eyes never left her. "Will you just tell me? Whatever it is, I'll deal with it."

Her face burned. He had no idea what he was saying. She could barely deal with it. No one else should have to. Even though her mom would someday have to help her, take care of her, she wished to God she could spare her mom from it again. "I don't want you to deal with it," she spat. "It's mine to deal with, not yours."

"Okay, I'm sorry," he said, finally looking away. "I just wanted to help."

Maddy wanted to scream because if she screamed, she wouldn't cry, but he didn't deserve to be yelled at anymore. "You can't. Nobody can." She glanced in the direction of his bedroom, wishing her things were packed instead of strewn across the floor in his room. "I need to leave, and you need to let me leave. I know I said we could go to the Rainbow Gathering together, but I need to do this alone."

When she looked at him—at the hurt and confusion on his face—she wished she hadn't. "What's changed?" he asked. "A few minutes ago, we were talking about packing for the gathering. I thought we had plans—"

She held up her hand. "No strings. You promised."

He looked like he wanted to yell at her, then his shoulders drooped in defeat. "Yeah, no fucking strings," he muttered.

Tears blurred her vision while she got dressed and stuffed her clothes in her backpack to the sound of Duncan sweeping up the broken glass. Then she grabbed her things from the bathroom and shoved them into her bag. Before she went back to the kitchen, she took some time to wipe away her tears and pull herself together. She took a deep breath and told herself that leaving now was better. If it were this hard to walk away from him now, it would be that much worse if they'd gone to the gathering together.

Duncan was leaning against the couch, his arms crossed, when she walked out with her things. "Will you at least tell me what it is?" he asked in a quiet voice.

"Why?" She tried to keep her voice from shaking. "I'm leaving. It doesn't matter."

"I just want to know."

She was about to turn toward the door but stopped. She'd already broken almost every rule with him. It wouldn't matter if he knew now because she never planned to see him again. "I'll tell you, but it's not going to change anything. I, um…" She hadn't said the words out loud since she'd told her mom, and then Keith, a year ago. "I have Huntington's Disease."

He shook his head. "I don't know what that is."

"Huntington's Chorea. My dad died from it, and so will I."

The devastated look on his face made her feel awful. "Don't be sad for me, Duncan, please don't. This trip—it's about living, not about being sick. And this week… It was… It…" She swallowed against the lump in her chest threatening to rise into her throat and choke her. "These were some of the best days I've had since I found out." It took everything she had not to go to him, to hug him, to stay with him. "Thanks for that."

He moved toward her. "Maddy, wait."

She shook her head and went to the door. "Bye, Duncan," she whispered and closed the door behind her.

At least he respected her wishes and didn't follow her.

Maddy didn't know where to go. The only places she knew of were the places she and Duncan had gone together. She didn't want to relive those memories or chance running into him.

She ended up going to the college campus and found a secluded spot under a tree where she spent most of the day. She read a little, played her guitar a little, then took a nap in the afternoon. If only her car was fixed. Then she could drive away, take her time getting to Utah, even go to the gathering early. From what she'd read online, people were already there as part of a seed camp, setting up kitchens, establishing trails.

By the time the sun began to set, Maddy was exhausted and miserable. She thought about staying put and sleeping beneath the tree, but throughout the day, campus security had come by a few times. The last time, the security officer walked by slower, looking at her longer, giving her the message that he'd noticed her sitting there most of the day.

It was one of the first times on her journey that she felt truly lonely. She needed something, someplace that was familiar, so she pulled out her phone and checked the public transportation schedule.

Forty minutes later, she walked the few blocks from the bus stop to Bernie's Auto Shop, took out her spare set of keys, and climbed into her car. As chilly as it was, there was immense comfort within the tiny space of her car. It had been with her through everything. Through graduating from med school, to her excitement about her residency, to the devastation of her diagnosis, to saying goodbye to Keith, and finally, this journey. She talked to her car, sang at the top of her lungs, hashed out her frustrations. It held so much of her. It was because of her car that she met Duncan.

Maddy shook her head, trying to push him out of it. She untied her sleeping bag from her backpack and draped it over her, then leaned her seat back. Even though it sometimes got into the 80s during the day, the temperature often dipped into the fifties at night. At least she had a good sleeping bag that would keep her warm.

Hopefully she could just fall asleep and block out the day. She set her phone alarm for 6:00 a.m. so she'd be up and gone from Bernie's by the time anyone got to the auto shop.

##

A knock on her car window startled her out of sleep. A hint of light pushed through the darkness, signaling the early morning. She panicked, thinking her alarm hadn't gone off or that Bernie came to work much earlier than she thought he would. She sat up, trying to figure out what she would tell him.

It wasn't Bernie at her window. It was Duncan standing there in a T-shirt and jeans, shivering. Seeing him brought back every moment they'd spent together. Her heart danced with the memories, each one like a piece of a song woven together until it formed something beautiful. Then she remembered why she left.

She should have been mad that he'd found her, but he looked so worried, so miserable, she just felt bad. She cracked her door open to talk to him. "What are you doing?"

"I was worried about you." He rubbed his arms like he was trying to get warm. "I just—I want to talk."

"We already talked."

He shook his head. "You talked. I didn't get to."

He was right. When she looked at it from his side of things, it felt pretty shitty. "Get in here," she sighed.

He jogged around to the passenger's side and got in, his breath joining with hers, creating a layer of fog on the windows. Duncan huddled down in his seat and crossed his arms for warmth. Maddy turned her sleeping bag sideways and handed him an end of it.

"Thanks," he mumbled.

They sat in silence for a minute. He ran his fingers along the sleeping bag zipper like he was searching for something. Finally, he looked at her. "I read about it," he said in a quiet voice. "About Huntington's."

She nodded. "Me too." She'd gone down that rabbit hole several times—after her dad was diagnosed, and again after she'd tested positive for the gene.

"There's really no cure?" he asked with just a sliver of hope in his voice.

"Not yet. Probably not anytime soon."

He looked down "I'm sorry. I'm… I don't know what to say."

His discomfort reminded her why she didn't tell people about her disease. "You don't have to say anything. And you don't need to be here. You don't owe me anything."

A flash of anger crossed his eyes when he looked at her. "Do you really think that's why I'm here? Because of some messed up sense of obligation?"

"I don't know," she shot back at him. "But this is why I don't tell people. It just muddies the water and complicates things. Would you even be here right now if I made up some lie about why I had to leave?”

“That’s not fair—”

“Fair?!” She’d come to hate that word. “Nothing is fair! You don’t get to talk to me about what’s fair and what’s not.” Every meditation and mindfulness technique she’d ever practiced was pulverized under the weight of that word. She’d tried so hard not to dwell on unanswerable questions like *why her, why her dad, why anyone?*

She thought she might have scared Duncan away, but instead of leaving, something seemed to shift in him and he settled into his seat, no longer looking fidgety. “How long have you known?”

“What?” His question caught her off guard.

“How long have you known you’ve had Huntington’s?”

She was surprised by his directness. When her dad got sick, most people sidestepped the subject or talked around it, like avoiding it would make everyone forget that he’d been given a death sentence.

As much as Maddy thought she didn’t want to talk about it, the words tumbled out of her like they’d been pushing against her throat, waiting to get out. “For a little over a year,” she said. “I didn’t want to know for a long time. The whole time my dad was sick I refused to get tested, even though I knew I had a fifty percent chance of having it. I just wanted to live my life like normal and see what happened, but then...” She pictured Keith’s face—his black hair and dark eyes. They met on the first day of her internship, both wanting to become cardiothoracic surgeons. It felt like a lifetime ago. It was.

"Then I was with someone and it got pretty serious and we were talking about marriage and kids someday, and I—I couldn't just blindly go into that without knowing. I saw what my mom went through with my dad." She remembered her dad, trapped and tortured in a body that was bedridden, a body that wouldn't let him talk or laugh or play music. The disease stole everything that made him who he was. "She watched him die for almost fifteen years, a slow, horrific death that stole both of their lives." Her voice caught, but she kept going. "I won't put anyone through that. My mom…she'll be a casualty of it again. As much as I don't want her to be, she'll insist." She shook her head. "But nobody else."

Duncan looked down, making it impossible to read his face. "And this guy you were with—he just let you decide for him?" he asked, sounding irritated.

She let out a frustrated sigh. "It wasn't like that. He said he wanted to do the right thing, be supportive, stay with me, but I didn't want that for him. He was brilliant and had an amazing future ahead of him as a surgeon."

"He just left?"

"Yeah, and he should have." She pictured her dad again. "You don't know how hard it is to watch someone you know, someone you love die that way."

He surprised her by putting his hand on hers. "You could tell me," he whispered.

When she met Duncan almost a week ago, she never imagined that she'd trust him with the deepest pain in her life. She told him about feeling helpless while she watched her dad suffer for fifteen years—physically, emotionally, mentally—

while the disease slowly stole his life. "The worst part was seeing what it did to him, to know how much he suffered. And when it got to the point where he couldn't tell us what was wrong, it was—" She took in a shaky breath. "You could tell he was just tortured, but we could only guess at how to help him, to make him more comfortable. I watched this beautiful, vibrant man waste away until all he could do was lay in bed. He couldn't even talk anymore."

She wiped her eyes and leaned back, feeling exhausted.

He squeezed her hand. "God, Maddy, I'm so sorry."

She nodded, trying to force her tears to stop. "Believe me, I don't want to die, especially like that, but I'm sadder for my mom than I am for me. She deserves sainthood. She shouldn't ever have to—" She choked back a sob. "She doesn't deserve this."

"Neither do you," he said, his voice thick with emotion.

"A lot of good that does me," she snapped. "The damn disease doesn't care who gets it, so I'm finding my own way to deal with it."

He brushed some of her tears away with his thumb. "You don't have to do it alone."

She pulled back from him. "Don't."

Don't what?" He looked bewildered.

"Don't get all noble and play the part of the hero who's going to swoop down and rescue me. This is why I don't tell people." She clenched her fists. "It changes things. People treat me differently."

"That's not fair."

She shook her head and clenched her jaw. "Now we're back to fair?"

He looked at her, his eyes fierce. "Yeah we are. You have no idea how I'll react or how I'm going to treat you, so don't assume you know."

"You can't tell me it won't change things!" Her voice cracked through the chilly air, but he didn't retreat.

"It might change a few things," he conceded, "but it's not going to change how I am with you." He leaned forward and put his hand on hers again. "After everything you've told me yesterday and today, you know what I want to do?"

"What?" She expected his answer to be something about holding her, taking care of her, protecting her.

"I want us to go back to my apartment and scrounge up whatever shitty breakfast we can find. Then I want to go back to bed like we do almost every morning because god knows I can't ever get enough of you and me in bed together. Sometime during the day we can pack for the Rainbow Gathering. We could play at the Pearl Street Mall later, or just head back to bed again."

There was no hint of a lie on his face or in his voice. As much as she wanted to deny her own truth, her own feelings, Duncan deserved to hear it. It would make her life messier, less predictable, but she didn't come on this journey to play it safe.

Her heart thundered with nervous energy. "This wasn't supposed to happen," she said.

He shook his head, looking confused. "What wasn't supposed to happen?"

She turned to him. "You, dammit—staying with you, liking you. I told myself I wasn't going to hook up with anyone on this trip, and I definitely wasn't going to get attached to anyone."

"Wait, you mean you haven't… I just assumed you—that there were other—"

She couldn't stop herself from laughing at his reaction. "So you didn't believe me when I told you I didn't sleep around? You think this trip is just a sex fest?"

He put his hand up in defense. "No, but I thought there must have—that there were at least a few—" He shook his head. "I couldn't have fucked that up any worse."

"Probably not."

"Thanks," he said sarcastically. "I just meant that you seem like you're someone who lives in the moment, so I assumed there were other people, other moments."

She took his hand in both of hers and held his gaze. "No. It was a rule I had, a rule I stuck to." The connection she'd felt the first time they sang together flooded her. It was a connection that permeated everything, from talking, to playing music, to making love. "And then I met you."

He looked away from her. "You make it sound like a bad thing."

"My life would be easier if we hadn't met. So would yours."

He was quiet for a few moments, then he looked at her again. "Easier, but not better."

The honesty in his blue eyes pulled at her, even stronger than before. He knew the truth now, but he didn't want to run away or rescue her. He'd shown her his heart over and over. It was time to show him hers.

"You know, I didn't want to like you," she said, leaning closer to him, their lips almost touching.

His breath brushed her cheek. "But then?"

The only way to answer was to kiss him. It was a deep, beautiful kiss, flavored with everything they'd shared over the past week. By the time they pulled away from each other, every window was layered in fog, obscuring the sunrise.

"Let's go," Maddy whispered.

"Where?"

"To do everything you said you wanted to do today. You know, breakfast, bed…music, bed…packing, bed."

He smiled the carefree smile she loved.

They grabbed her things from her car and Maddy locked the doors. She headed toward Duncan's car, but he reached out and stopped her. "Now I know why you named your car Woody Guthrie."

She nodded. Woody Guthrie had died because of Huntington's. He'd fought hard against it, staying active in music and social justice issues as long as he possibly could. "He's my hero in a lot of ways."

"I can see why."

She grabbed his hand. "Duncan?"

"What?"

"Promise me this won't change things between us. I don't want things to get too heavy or weird."

He shook his head. "You're still you and I'm still me, so I think we'll be okay as long as we remember that."

She put her guitar down and hugged him. "You're kind of brilliant…for a musician."

##

Maddy didn't need to worry about things changing between them. Nothing changed about the way they made love when they got back to his apartment. If anything, she felt freer.

They lay together afterward and talked more about the Rainbow Gathering.

"I don't know what we're supposed to do," Maddy said, thinking beyond the gathering.

Duncan lay behind her, his arms around her waist. "What do you mean?"

"After the gathering. There's still so much I want to do and see. And you have a life here, so…"

He kissed her shoulders, sending trails of warmth through her skin. "We don't have to figure everything out right now. Going to the gathering might help us figure it out."

She liked the way that sounded. "I'm okay taking things day by day if you are. I don't like to make too many plans."

"I kind of figured that."

She laughed, then yawned—a yawn so big it stretched through her entire body. "I slept like shit last night," she said, trying to stifle a second yawn.

"You can sleep now if you want to."

She glanced at the digital clock which read 1:05. "It's the middle of the day. Besides, we need to pack."

He pulled her closer. "To hell with plans, right?"

She settled into the warmth radiating from him. "Right," she said in a sleepy voice.

He kissed her head, then whispered, "Don't laugh."

"I'll try not to," she whispered back, wondering what he was talking about.

A moment later, he began to sing "Hobo's Lullaby" to her, a song that Woody Guthrie recorded. The haunting lyrics were about finding a moment of peace in a world that was often too cruel. She closed her eyes and melted into the song.

This, right now, in bed with Duncan was her moment of peace. Her hobo's lullaby.

CALL ME RAIN

Wednesday, June 24

Elaine had waited years for this day. For the last six years she'd thrown herself into her work, and today it paid off. A local hospital board had selected her design out of all the others presented to them for a new suburban hospital. Today she and several other architects working on the project were presenting the final blueprints to the board. If they approved it, they'd break ground later in the summer.

Dave, the department head, poked his head in her office door. "You need anything before the meeting?"

A Xanax would help. As excited as she was, she was also sleep deprived, which made her more anxious than normal. Instead of admitting her nerves, Elaine sat up straighter. "No, everything's ready to go."

"You know, the way Emmitt talks about you, you'll have my job in no time."

Elaine brushed him off with a wave of her hand, but inside she swelled with pride. She'd risen from the ranks of entry level intern to Architect/Designer II faster than anyone else in the firm had. It didn't take long for the senior partner, Emmitt, to notice her talent and take a personal interest in her career.

"I don't think you have anything to worry about," she told Dave.

"Well, all eyes are on you today."

She raised her eyebrows at him. "Nothing like being in the hot seat."

"You'll be fine. I'll see you in fifteen minutes." He gave her a thumbs up and walked down the hall.

Elaine stared out her office window at her view of New York City. Everything about her life there these past six years had been exactly what she'd hoped for. Except for the loneliness. Her long hours at work meant she didn't have much of a social life. It was harder than she thought it would be to make real friends, to actually get close to someone. She'd thought about calling her mom to tell her about taking the lead role in designing the hospital, but they didn't talk much anymore, and Elaine doubted that any of her accomplishments would mean much to her mom.

Her phone rang, breaking through her thoughts.

She tucked her auburn hair behind her ears and picked it up. "Elaine Kennedy," she said.

"Rain?"

Elaine pulled the phone away from her ear for a moment, caught off guard by the name. Her mom was the only one who still called her Rain. It wasn't even her legal name anymore.

Her chest tightened. "Who is this?"

"It's, um, it's Campbell. I don't know if you remember—"

His voice, his name threw her back in time. She was ten, playing in the little river, building a dam with sticks.

Campbell handed her another stick, looking at her dam with admiration. "You think it will hold?" he asked.

She carefully placed the stick, securing it. "Better than the one you built." She tossed her head in the direction of the remnants of his dam that was in ruins on the other side of the river.

He laughed. She liked that about him, that he could laugh at himself. Her childhood friend, her best friend.

Until he wasn't.

She hadn't talked to him since they were eighteen. "Campbell?" How did he get her number at work? "What—why—?" Nothing made sense.

"There's something I need to tell you."

He paused for a moment, a pause that made her palms sweat and her stomach twist. It had to be about her mom, but she'd talked to her mom a month ago and her mom was…well, she was her mom.

"What did she do? Did she get arrested at a protest or something?"

"No." Campbell's voice was soft, almost a whisper. "She's…she passed away."

The words didn't feel real. They couldn't be. Her mom was only fifty. She was a health nut who lived off the grid, who lived off the land.

"Rain?"

She should have felt something. Sadness or anger or something, but there was nothing.

"Rain? Are you there?"

The name finally made her feel something. It scratched at her like an itchy sweater she couldn't wait to shed. "That's not my name anymore."

"What?" Campbell sounded shocked. "Did you hear me? About your mom?"

"Yeah." She was still numb. "How—what happened?"

He took a shaky breath. "It looked like she was on a ladder and fell and hit her head. I found her yesterday."

"Yesterday? And you're just calling me now?"

"It took me that long to find you."

She closed her eyes and massaged her forehead, trying to convince herself this wasn't happening.

"There are things you need to take care of," Campbell said in a gentle voice. "You need to come home."

She glanced out at the city again. This was home now.

"Okay," she whispered, then ended the call.

The knock on her office door made her jump. She looked up to see the office manager, Linda, in the doorway. "The board just got here," Linda said, glancing toward the conference room down the hall.

"I—I, um, I don't know what to do," Elaine said in a voice that didn't feel like her own. "My mother just died." Was she supposed to go to the meeting? Was she supposed to leave for Colorado now? Nothing felt real. Nothing felt right.

##

Elaine drove her rental Jeep out of the hotel parking lot just after sunrise. She'd flown into Durango, Colorado last night, but was too tired, too overwhelmed to go to her mom's place after her flight.

She'd gotten Campbell's number from the caller ID at work but hadn't gathered the energy or courage to call him. Instead, she'd sent him a text, letting him know when she was flying in. He texted back, telling her he could meet her at her mom's this morning before he headed to work.

She grabbed the steaming travel mug of coffee and took a drink, hoping the caffeine would chase away the extra dose of Xanax she'd taken last night. Needing more than coffee to wake up, she rolled her windows down as she drove out of Durango.

The San Juan Mountains stood in the distance in front of her. She'd forgotten how commanding, how beautifully intimidating they were. She sucked in a breath of the sharp, cold morning air. There was a hint of pine mixed with the fresh crystalline smell of snow that still blanketed the tallest peaks of the San Juans. The smells carried unwanted memories, unwanted emotions that were impossible to reconcile. How could she love and hate a place so much? It made her want to turn around, to turn her back on the mountains, and fly back to New York.

A few miles outside of Durango, Elaine left the highway for county roads that eventually led to the half mile gravel lane leading to her mom's place.

She stopped at the far end of the lane, trying to slow her breathing, her pounding pulse. She gripped the steering wheel to keep her hands from shaking and put her foot on the gas.

Tall pines lined the lane, shielding it from the road, giving the illusion that her mom's acreage was 150 miles from civilization instead of fifteen. When the simple one and a half story log home came into view, Elaine wanted to turn around. It looked the same as it did when she'd last seen it in the rearview mirror right after high school graduation ten years ago. It was the last time she'd been home.

Elaine shook her head. This wasn't home anymore.

As she pulled up to the house, memories of her childhood, of her mom, left her breathless. Her mom was in every log, every shingle, every acre of land. It wasn't just her mom—this place held everything Elaine used to be. The person she'd tried to leave behind.

She parked and tried to swallow her emotions. But when she got out of her car and saw the front door open, her knees almost buckled. For a fraction of a second, she expected her mom to step onto the porch and welcome her home, her arms outstretched, ready to hold her, to tell Elaine how sorry she was.

The vision evaporated as a man stepped out of the house. It took her a moment to place him. He was still tall, but he was no longer the skinny kid he'd been years ago. He'd filled out, his lean muscles visible beneath his grey T-shirt. His chocolate brown hair was pulled back in a bun.

It looked like it took him a few seconds to recognize her too, but she couldn't blame him. Her once frizzy, wild auburn hair was tamed and smooth thanks to her flat iron. She couldn't remember the last time she'd gone barefoot or had worn tattered cut-offs.

Then he smiled, and he was Campbell. She wanted to go to him, to put her arms around him, to feel the friendship they'd once shared. Instead, she stayed glued to her spot. Their friendship was old. Old and dissolved. But Campbell walked toward her like she was still his friend. She thought he might wrap her in his famous bear hug, but he stopped when he reached her, looking unsure.

"Hey," he said, scuffing the gravel with his hiking boot.

"Hey."

"It's, um, it's good to see you."

"Yeah, you too." She bit her lip to keep it from quivering. The long flight, her broken sleep, being here, seeing Campbell—it all caught up to her.

"I'm so sorry about your mom." This time he did reach out to her. She met him in an awkward one-armed hug. Before he pulled away, she caught the smell of sawdust and the musky hint of sweat.

"You want to go inside?" he asked after he'd pulled away.

"No." She wasn't ready for that. It was hard enough to set foot on the property. She'd need to get her bearings before she went in the house. "Let's sit on the porch."

They sat side by side on the wide porch steps. Elaine's gaze traveled to the barn and the little fenced paddock that surrounded it. A goat and a cow munched on some hay while two horses gazed over the fence as if they were daydreaming about freedom. There was no sound aside from a few birds and a vocal squirrel. The absence of noise was unnerving.

"You can stay here if you want to," Campbell said.

No, she couldn't. "Does she have electricity yet? Internet?"

"No, you know your mom. She'd die before she'd poison this place with electricity." He shook his head and looked sick. "Sorry, I didn't mean—"

She wanted to reassure him, to squeeze his hand, but she kept hers in her lap. "It's okay. She might still be here if she had a phone, someone she could have called for help when she fell."

The color left Campbell's tan face. "It wouldn't have mattered. I don't think she could have called for help. I just wish…" He swallowed. "If I'd checked in on her early in the week, then maybe… Fuck." He put his face in his hands.

It felt natural to put her hand on his back, to try to comfort him. "I'm sorry you had to find her."

He leaned forward and put his elbows on his knees. "I came here every Saturday. She'd make a big lunch and we'd spend the afternoon doing whatever projects she needed help with. I stopped by on Wednesday with a few things I'd picked up for her and she was…" His shoulders slumped. "I wish I would have known. I don't know how long she lay there or if she suffered, or…"

Elaine tried to shake the image of her mom lying on the floor with no one to help her. "You had no way of knowing this would happen."

He shook his head. "Still, no one should die alone."

His statement sent splinters of ice through her, making her shiver. Despite their differences, despite the chasm between them, Elaine couldn't stand the thought of her mom suffering, dying alone.

Everything hit her at once—her mom's death, being back here, sitting next to someone who was so familiar, but now a stranger. It was too much to deal with, making her feel lightheaded, like she was headed for a panic attack. She needed to leave, to get back to her world. "What do I need to do? What do I have to take care of before I go back to New York? I can't stay long."

He looked a little put off by what she'd said. "There's a lot you need to do. I don't think your mom had things in order. Well, not in any organized way. She'd told me once that there were some papers in her old family journal, but I didn't think it was my place to look for them."

Elaine bowed her head. "This is going to be a disaster, isn't it. I can't stay here and sort through her stuff." More like she couldn't sort through the memories and the heartache. *I don't know who you are…you're not my daughter.*

She stole a glance at Campbell and remembered their childhood, playing in the river, riding horses, camping under the stars. Not all the memories were bad.

"There's no one else to do it, Rain."

She let out a frustrated breath. "That's not my name anymore, it's Elaine." She'd changed it right after college, worried that no one in the professional world would take her seriously with a name like Rain.

"Sorry," he sighed. "I can't get used to that. Your mom told me you'd changed your name."

Did she talk about me a lot? Did she miss me? Was she sorry? The words died before they made it to her lips. The answers might destroy her.

She bounced her knee, needing to move, needing some kind of release. "Is there someone who can take care of the place for now? Someone to feed the animals? I could pay them. I don't know anything about this place anymore."

"It hasn't changed that much." He nodded at the animals in the paddock. "They just need food and water every day. The gardens need to be weeded and watered, but we can probably let them go for a day or two.

A few days. She planned to be back in New York in a few days.

Campbell sighed. "If you give me a couple of days, I can find someone to help with the animals and the land, but right now, it's up to you and me." He looked in the direction of the barn. "I can show you what the animals need."

He stood and offered her his hand. She took it and felt his strong, calloused hand around hers, but as soon as she got up, it was gone. It had been a long time since anyone had taken her hand. She didn't date much, hadn't had a serious boyfriend for two years. She had a few short flings, but flings didn't lend themselves to hand holding, to intimacy.

When they reached the barn, the smell of hay, oats, and leather horse tack transported her back to every summer, every weekend when she couldn't wait to get out of bed and take her horse out for a ride. Even in the winter, she'd bundle up and ride her horse bareback through the pasture and down to the river that separated her mom's land from Campbell's parents' place. He'd usually meet her there later, but the early mornings were hers.

As soon as Elaine and Campbell reached the barn, the two horses, the cow, and the goat made a mad dash to the barn door. All four of them were fat and sleek. "It doesn't look like they ever miss a meal," she said.

Campbell laughed. "That's for sure. They're just a little spoiled. But they deserve it after what they've been through."

Elaine couldn't stop herself from smiling. "She rescued them, didn't she."

He nodded. "Like always."

They fed the animals in silence, and she got lost in the physical work of getting hay from the loft and filling the grain bins and water tanks. It had been ten years since she'd done it, but after a few minutes, it felt just as natural now as it did then.

"Your mom said you're an architect?" Campbell said as he raked the loose hay from the barn aisle.

She sat on a hay bale. "Yeah. It was tough for a while, working my way up, but I work for an amazing firm. They really value me...my work."

He sat beside her and looked out the window like he was looking back in time. "You were always better at designing stuff than I was."

A memory crept through her mind, making her smile. "Remember that cabin we wanted to build by the river?"

He chuckled. "Just like the pioneers."

"It was doomed before it started. How old were we? Ten?"

"Something like that." When he looked at her, she'd forgotten how rich his brown eyes were—dark like his hair, but always filled with emotion or questions. "You know what's funny?" he asked.

"What?" She made herself look away from his eyes.

"I build things for a living now."

Laughter tumbled out of her. "You? Really? The guy whose fort couldn't stand up to the slightest breeze?"

He nudged her shoulder. "Go ahead and rub it in, but believe it or not, I'm pretty damn good at it now. I've got my own business as a contractor. I help people build green homes and tiny houses. I've even helped some people get completely off the grid."

His career path didn't surprise her. He'd been fascinated by the way she and her mom lived from the first day he came to their house when they were in first grade. They'd been inseparable after that with him spending much more time at her place than she ever did at his parents' house. But by the time they were in high school, he was still enamored with the way they lived, while Elaine felt suffocated by it. No electricity meant no television or stereo or computer. All the work it took to run the house and the gardens meant no social life. Everything was a pain in the ass including cooking and food storage. It wasn't the kind of life she wanted.

"I bet my mom was proud of you," she said.

He gave her a sad smile and nodded. "My parents wanted me to do something more, but I always knew I wanted to do something with my hands." He looked at her, then his gaze dropped. "She was proud of you too."

You're not my daughter. Elaine stood up, feeling like she'd been punched. "Don't," she said. "If you knew…" It all came back to her, bubbling up from the dust and dirt. "It was pretty clear that I was a disappointment, a sellout."

He stood and put his hand on her shoulder. "Rain…"

She shrugged his hand away. "My name's Elaine!" She moved away from him and paced the barn aisle. "I shouldn't have come back, I should have had a lawyer take care of things. Just…just tell me what I need to do so I can get out of here. I can't stay here."

"Okay," he said in a soft voice, like he was talking to a scared animal. "We'll figure it out. The most important thing right now is the funeral or some kind of service."

Her stomach lurched, making her feel like she might throw up. A funeral would mean seeing her mom again. It would make things too real.

She always thought there'd be time to mend things, but Elaine's life had gotten too busy to come back to Colorado, even though she sometimes promised to try. But her mom could have tried too. She could have gotten on a plane and come to New York, even for a weekend.

Now any chance to reconnect was dead. There was just a blanket of regret that covered all the things they'd never get to talk about.

"Where's—where is she? What funeral home?" she asked, trying to turn off her emotions. She needed to get back to the hotel, to take a Xanax, have a glass or two of wine.

"She's at Kramer's funeral home. Jack Kramer knew her pretty well. He'll know what she'd want in a service. I can help if you want me to."

She sat on the haybale again, worried she'd lose her footing. "She won't want a funeral."

Campbell nodded. "Not a traditional one. I told Jack that she'd probably want to be cremated, but he needs to hear it from you."

She leaned forward and put her head in her hands, trying to make the world stop. "Will I…" She tried to swallow the fear, the guilt. "Will I get to see her?"

Campbell's hand was on her back, strong and soothing. "She'd been gone for a few days when I found her, so she didn't look very good." He took his hand away and wrapped his arms around himself. "There's only so much the funeral home could have done to make her look…" He shook his head and stood up. "You shouldn't see her like that. No one should. You should just remember her how she was."

How she was… The mother who loved her with a fierceness. The mother who beamed at seven-year-old Rain working beside her in the garden, building fences, baking homemade bread, canning food for the winter, stoking the fire. But that love seemed to shift after Elaine longed for something more, something different.

She turned to Campbell. "Does she really need a service or memorial? Can't we just skip it and scatter her ashes? She'd want to be here in the land—that much I know." As soon as she said it, she felt bad. The word "we" had come out so easily, like they were still a team, still best friends. She doubted Campbell felt that way anymore.

He didn't seem to notice her word choice. "Your mom wouldn't care about a service, but she touched a lot of lives and I think people would want to honor her, celebrate her."

"Okay," she sighed. "I guess I should go see Jack Kramer, set a date, find out what he needs me to do. Then I'll call a lawyer I know, see if she can help me settle the estate since I doubt Mom had an official will or anything."

She was surprised to feel Campbell's hand on hers. "Or you could wait a few days and see if she left anything here for you…a will or something. I can help you."

She pulled her hand away. "You know, I'm not helpless. I'm perfectly capable of taking care of things."

He stood and moved away from her, his gaze fixed on the open barn window. "I've never thought you were helpless. I'm offering because I loved your mom. She was one of the most important people in my life. You should know that more than anyone."

She wanted to apologize, but she stood there, trapped by jealousy and guilt. It was obvious how close Campbell and her mom were, making her wonder if he'd taken her place.

He looked at her like he was waiting for her to say something. When she didn't, he gave her a resigned look and shook his head. "Will you at least let me know when the service is?" he asked.

"Okay."

He walked out of the barn without saying anything else to her, leaving her alone.

Sunday, June 28

Elaine spent the next two days trying to prepare for her mom's celebration of life. That's what she and Jack Kramer had agreed to call it. Jack told her to bring pictures and personal items, anything that would show who her mom was.

She'd started to gather pictures, pieces of the mosaic of her mom's life. There were other things—pottery, a few paintings. As she looked through desk drawers and closets and photo albums, Elaine's life tumbled out of every page and shelf and drawer—a happy toddler in the garden covered in dirt, a delighted grin on her face. An eight-year-old riding the big draft horse they'd had. She and Campbell showing off the fort they'd built by the river.

It was strange to see herself so happy, really happy. Everything that happened since high school had clouded that happiness, erased some of its purity. When was the last time she'd felt truly happy? Was it in the picture of her and Campbell at one of the local summer music festivals? They must have been about fourteen, the summer before they started high school.

She grabbed all the pictures in the desk drawer and shoved them in an envelope, but the memories pulled at her, reminding her of a mother who loved her, who let her be free and wild, who wanted her to find meaning and happiness in the world. But how could she reconcile those memories with the mom who was so disappointed in her, the mom who no longer understood her.

As she gathered up pieces of her mom's life, she wanted to call Campbell. He was a part of that life, woven just as tightly into it as Elaine was, but she didn't want to need him. She'd only contacted him once in the last two days, texting him the date and time of the service.

He was there when she got to Kramer's funeral home, two hours before the service was supposed to start. He'd brought pictures of his own that were set up in collages and frames, not stuffed in a big envelope like hers.

"I, um, I had some things I wanted to bring," he said, shifting his weight. "Just a few pictures. I didn't know what you'd bring."

She held out the big manila envelope. "I don't know what to do with these. I guess I should have arranged them or something."

"We've got some time. I'm sure Jack has some poster board or something we can use to display them."

She reached out and touched his arm. "Thanks." She wanted to thank him for being there, for letting the past go, at least for the moment. He was always a better person than she was.

Elaine didn't expect many people to show up. They had no extended family anywhere nearby. Elaine never knew her father. All she knew about him was that he didn't want to be a father, so he was never a part of her life.

She honestly thought she and Campbell would be the only people there, but during the two-hour span of the celebration, a steady stream of people came through. Elaine remembered a few of them from her childhood, but most she'd never met. Everyone who talked to Elaine had stories to tell about her mom—her mom's goodness, the way she'd help anyone who needed a hot meal or some clothes or a place to stay.

Elaine had never heard these stories, had never seen that part of her mom's life. Her mom always had a big heart, but Elaine had no idea she'd touched so many lives.

By the time the service was over, Elaine was exhausted. She'd had to shut off her emotions during the day. It was the only way she could deal with her mom's service, her mom's death. She had no idea how exhausting it was to numb herself.

Jack Kramer walked over to where she sat on one of the couches. "I can help you gather this stuff up." He patted her shoulder. "You look tired. You should go home and get some rest."

Home. The word seeped into her skin and clung to her heart, squeezing it, making it ache. "Home?" Her voice shook. "I don't… I don't have a home." She wrapped her arms around herself. "God, I don't even have a home anymore."

Campbell was there beside her as if he'd magically materialized. He sat down and took her hand. Somehow he knew not to say anything, that his hand on hers, his presence beside her meant more than anything he could have said.

Finally she sucked in a breath and sat up straighter. "I'm sorry, I—I didn't expect—"

"I know." The honesty in his voice told her what he'd lost too.

Jack came back, giving her a welcome interruption. "I put your pictures and everything else on the table out front."

She nodded. "Thanks for everything, Jack."

"Your mom was a special person."

"I know," she sighed. A special person Elaine had been too busy, too hurt to get close to again. Too busy—it was a terrible excuse.

Campbell squeezed her hand. "Do you want help taking this stuff to your car?"

"Yeah, but I want to take it back to my mom's place now. I can't—I don't want it sitting in my car."

"I can drive you," Campbell said, "then I'll give you a ride back here to get your car."

"I'll be okay." She didn't want to inconvenience him. He'd already done too much.

"You look exhausted, Ra—Elaine. I don't know if you should drive."

She nodded. He was probably right.

##

When they got to her mom's place, it was dark enough that they had to light some oil lamps. The soft glow and shadows from the lamps played on the walls. A cool evening wind wafted through the window, bringing in a hint of the mountains, a hint of wildness. When she looked at Campbell, who stood beside her in the kitchen, she was propelled back in time to where they'd stood in almost the same spot, the windows open, craving adventure and freedom.

The memory made her smile, lifting a bit of the grief, the heaviness from the day. "This brings back memories," she said.

Campbell gave her a soft smile, making her wonder which memories had come to his mind. "Summers were the best," he said.

"She gave us a lot of freedom, probably trusted us more than she should have."

"Yeah," he chuckled. "Did she ever notice the missing wine?"

"If she did, she never said anything." She put a hand to her forehead. "Trust me, my hangover was punishment enough."

"Mine to."

"We thought we were so smart, so sneaky, no chance of being caught."

The flame from the oil lamp caught his dark eyes. "What were we? Fourteen?"

"Yep, we thought we were all grown up."

"Were we ever wrong," he said. "I never knew my head could hurt that bad. But that was some good wine."

"It was. Did she keep making it?"

Campbell nodded. "There are quite a few bottles in the root cellar." He grinned at her, the first real smile she'd seen from him all day.

A few minutes later, Campbell came back with a bottle of wine, popped the cork, and went to get glasses. Elaine grabbed his arm. "Come on, we don't need glasses." She took the bottle from him and slid down the wall to sit on the floor. He gave her a smile and sat beside her.

She took a long drink. It was the same sweet red wine she remembered. The taste of it brought back the summer days when she helped her mom make the wine. There was something about the process she loved.

The wine warmed her stomach. Some of it traveled to her head making her feel just a little lighter, a little mellower. She let out a long breath as if she'd been holding it all day, then passed the bottle to Campbell who took just as long of a drink.

"Who knew cheap wine could be this good," he said, and handed the bottle back to her.

"She was good at a lot of things, wasn't she?" Elaine didn't wait for him to answer. "She was really good at living this way…made it seem normal. I thought it was normal for a long time."

He gave her a half smile. "You know, living this way is natural, not abnormal. It's better in a lot of ways."

"Maybe." She didn't want to argue with him about it. She grabbed the bottle and took another drink. "Did you know she helped all those people?"

Campbell nodded. "After you left, I think it was her way of—I don't know—I just know she helped a lot of people. Did you find her box of postcards?"

"No." She had no idea what he was talking about.

"She helped anyone who needed it, whether they lived in Durango or were passing through. She was always bringing somebody back here to feed them or give them a place to sleep, a place to rest for a little while. Some people would stick around a few days or weeks and help her out in exchange for food and a place to stay. It was one of her dreams to do more, to find a way to help more people."

Her mom had always taken in stray animals. It was no surprise she'd gone on to take in stray people too.

"She's got a box full of postcards and letters from people who passed through, people whose lives she touched."

Elaine thought about her life, what it amounted to. People valued the work she did, but what did that work really mean? She designed commercial spaces. Even though her firm specialized in progressive and green spaces, it wasn't like she was designing homeless shelters or habitat for humanity houses. She designed buildings that cost millions to build, for corporations who were out to make money, even if they wanted to be environmentally conscious.

Her work wouldn't bring many people to her celebration of life.

She took another big gulp of wine.

"You might want to slow down a little," Campbell said, taking the bottle from her. Instead of putting it down, he took his own drink.

"Look who's talking," she shot back. "You're supposed to drive me back to town. I don't suppose Uber comes out here, do they?"

"I don't know, I guess we could find out." He looked around the kitchen. "Or you could stay here."

"Yes, because this is much more luxurious than my room at the Hilton."

He shook his head at her. "What happened to the girl who slept under the stars any chance she got?"

She remembered the thrill, the freedom of being outside, wrapped in her sleeping bag and blankets. There was something magical about staring up at millions of stars, realizing that people all over the world saw the same night sky. Those nights when she and Campbell camped together as kids were the best. Something about looking up at the stars made it easy to talk about anything and everything.

She tried to laugh off Campbell's question, tried to quiet the hint of wildness and freedom that pulled at her. "That girl got a Tempur-Pedic mattress and never looked back."

He nodded at a picture sitting on the cluttered bookcase. "You'd trade a soft mattress for that?"

She was probably seven when the picture was taken, her face painted with the colors of the rainbow. The smells of the forest, of bread baking in earthen ovens…the sound of guitars and banjos, of laughter, of voices calling out, "Welcome home" and "Lovin' you." The picture looked like it was from the gathering in Oregon.

"I haven't thought about Rainbow Gatherings in years," she said.

Campbell took another drink. "Do you have any idea how jealous I was every summer when you and your mom would go?"

"And every summer I hoped your parents would let you go."

He gave her a rueful smile. "My parents weren't crazy about all the time I spent here with 'that strange woman.' There was no way they'd let me go trekking off hundreds or thousands of miles to a Rainbow Gathering with her."

She took the wine from him and drank, enjoying the soft buzz. "You never went? Even as an adult?"

He shook his head. "I've been too busy building my business. Summer's my busiest time." He glanced at the picture again, then at the ceiling. "Your mom and I talked about going this year. It's up in Utah, only a day's drive."

"You should still do it." She closed her eyes, and for a moment she was back in a mountain meadow, her hands joined with fifteen thousand other people in silent meditation. She'd never known a more profound silence, a more profound connection with thousands of people who came together for a week and formed a community, a family.

He nudged her shoulder. "What about you? Aren't you curious to know what they're like now? If they're the same?"

A sliver of reality sliced through her warm buzz. "I couldn't go even if I wanted to. I've already been gone from work for too long. But you should go, Campbell. You'd love it, you really would."

He scooted closer to her and looked into her eyes, like he was searching for her. "*You* should go. It starts in a couple of days. It might be good for you to get away."

She almost said yes. If she'd had a little more wine, she might have. But she was still sober enough to know that if she

went to the gathering, there'd be no escaping from herself—
who she used to be, who she was now. You couldn't hide from
yourself at a Rainbow Gathering.

"I can't." She took the bottle and drank the last of the wine.
"I think we need more," she said as she stood up. She was more
buzzed than she thought she was, and had to sit back down.

"I'll get it," Campbell said. He was steadier on his feet than
she was, making her realize she'd probably had a lot more wine
than he had.

A few minutes later, he came back with another bottle and
opened it. He took a small drink, then sat beside her and
handed the bottle to her.

"This really does remind me of that night," she said.

He His brown eyes caught hers. "When we were
teenagers?"

"Yeah." She smiled at the memory. "We thought we were
so profound, talking about life and death and the meaning of it
all—how everything happens for a reason. We were so naïve."

The way he looked at her made her feel exposed,
vulnerable. "Yeah we were. I don't buy into that whole
'everything happens for a reason' crap anymore."

Maybe it was the wine or being so close to him, but she
longed to be closer. She leaned toward him until their shoulders
touched. "What do you buy into?" she asked.

He glanced at her, his eyes questioning. "I don't know,
especially after this happened to your mom. I don't know how
you make sense out of that. There are a lot of things I can't
make sense out of now, no matter how hard I try."

She looked away from him, not wanting to go too deep. "You should have been a philosophy major instead of a contractor."

His hand on hers made her look at him again. "I was being kind of serious, Ra—Elaine."

Those eyes…those deep brown eyes were still so intense. She'd always been drawn to them, to him. "You remember what else we did that night?"

A hint of recognition showed on his face. "Memories are strange things. We did a lot that night. Talked a lot, drank a lot."

She reached out and brushed his cheek with her fingers. "I asked you to kiss me."

He nodded. "You thought we should get practice for when we got girlfriends and boyfriends."

"I wanted you to be my first kiss," she whispered. "Someone I could trust, someone who'd be gentle."

He had been gentle. It had been awkward at first. Despite the wine, they were kids and they were nervous, fumbling as their lips first met. They'd laughed about it, then tried again. And again. And then it wasn't awkward. It was sweet and beautiful and it sent currents of warmth through her. She would have kissed him all night, but he was the one who'd stopped, saying they'd had enough practice.

"Can I tell you something?" Campbell asked, bringing her back to the present.

She nodded.

"I didn't want to practice," He took her hand that was still on his cheek and held onto it.

Although it was years ago, his words stung. She'd always thought he liked it. "What do you mean?"

"I wasn't interested in learning to kiss for some girlfriend." He leaned closer, close enough to feel his breath, close enough to hear the tiny tremor in his voice. "I wanted to kiss you."

She sighed and tilted her head. There was no fumbling, no awkwardness when their lips met now. His lips were gentle at first, barely brushing hers, then deepened with each kiss. His breath grew heavy, making her pulse thunder until it echoed in her ears.

It had been so long since she'd shared a connection with someone, every inch of her craved it. The strength of her need took her by surprise. There were no warm currents now. Her body burned with wanting him. She lay down and pulled him with her, pressing herself against him. A sigh escaped his lips, making her want him even more.

She took a moment to look at him, at the beauty in him, the beauty that was so much more than something physical. She smiled at him, a real smile that so rarely crossed her face anymore. "Hmmm," she said, staring at him. "You're kind of delicious."

He grinned back at her, but his eyes echoed her longing. "And you're kind of drunk."

"A little." She kissed him again. "But I'm sober enough to know that I want this." She leaned in and whispered in his ear, "I'm sober enough to know I won't regret it." She put her arms around the small of his back and pulled him as close as she could, loving the way he felt against her.

He let out a breath full of wanting, full of desire, then kissed her again.

She put her hands under his shirt reveling in the warmth of his skin, wishing they were naked together on the kitchen floor. "I want you," she whispered, tugging at his shirt, trying to pull it off.

As soon as she said it, something shifted in him. He stopped and sat up, his cheeks flushed, his breath heavy. "Not like this."

His rejection sliced through her like barbs. She moved away from him and crossed her arms. "Like what? What do you mean?"

He tried to take her hand, but she yanked it away. "Not when we've polished off almost two bottles of wine." His voice got softer. "And not on the same day we said goodbye to your mom."

She shook her head, furious at his chivalry, for thinking he was doing the right thing. "And what if this is what I need right now? Somebody to be close to. Somebody I care about."

He stood and looked at her, his eyes narrowed like he was trying to see inside of her. "This isn't just about you." He swallowed like something was wedged in his throat.

She had no idea what to say. She tried to sort out what he meant or what he might be thinking, but her head was too full and too fuzzy.

"We, uh, we should probably call it a night," he said, finally breaking the silence. "You want a ride to your hotel?"

She wanted her hotel, and a big part of her wanted him to be there with her. They could stay in bed and order room service, order some decent wine, pretend that the rest of the world didn't exist—just the two of them tangled together in bed.

One glance at him told her it wouldn't happen that way, that he'd just reject her again.

Elaine shook her head. She wasn't sure she could handle twenty minutes of awkwardness on the drive back to Durango. "I'm gonna stay here, sort through some things. I should find the family journal and go through it, see if she left anything resembling a will." It was something she'd been avoiding since she'd gotten there, but now it was even clearer that she needed to get back to New York.

"Okay," he sighed.

"Are you sure you should drive? That was a lot of wine."

He gave a small shake of his head. "You drank most of it, and I don't live that far away."

She realized she'd never asked him much about his life here now. All she knew was what he'd told her about being a contractor.

She scooted back and leaned against the wall. "Where do you live?"

"Just five miles up the road. I've got about eight acres where I built a tiny house."

"You never got married?" The words came out before she could stop them.

He took a step back and looked away from her. "I was engaged once, about three years ago, but it didn't work out."

The pain in his voice made her want to go to him, but he stood there stiff, barely looking at her.

"I'm sorry. I haven't—"

"Stop," he said, running a hand through his tangled hair. "I'm too tired to play twenty questions with you. It doesn't matter anyway. It's in the past." He turned and headed for the door. "If I don't see you before you leave, have a good trip back."

"Campbell," she called, but he didn't turn around. She almost asked him how she was supposed to get her rental car, but she didn't want to need anything from him. Instead, she wanted to scream at him for treating her worse than a stranger, especially after what they'd just shared, after how close they'd just been.

As soon as she heard his truck start, she hurled an empty wine bottle at the door, where it made a loud thud, then shattered when it hit the tile floor. "Fuck you! Fuck you and your eight acres and your fiancé and your shitty goodbyes! FUCK YOU ALL!"

She stumbled from the kitchen into the living room and made it to the couch. She pulled the quilt over her and tried to shut everything off so she wouldn't have to feel.

##

When Elaine woke, it was still dark outside, but the oil in the kitchen lamp had burned down quite a bit, telling her a few hours had passed. She picked up her phone which showed it was just after 4:00 a.m. A sliver of lightening sliced the sky followed by the soft rumble of thunder. Her head hurt when she sat up, an instant reminder of the wine and Campbell and what had happened between them. A reminder of why she needed to leave.

She lit the oil lamp sitting on the side table and carried it to the far corner of the living room to her mom's desk where she hoped to find the family journal. Once she knew if there was a will, she hoped she could leave and settle most of her mom's estate from New York. She might have to fly back once or twice to sign papers, but she could do a short day or overnight trip.

Finding the journal proved harder than she thought it would. The monstrous antique desk was in disarray with papers and records overflowing from drawers and compartments. There were financial records with the sales of her crops, essential oils, and natural cleaning supplies.

One drawer was full of pictures. More pictures from Rainbow Gatherings lay in the drawer. She pulled one out and smiled at the forgotten memory. Elaine was nine and she was holding a baby who'd just been born at the gathering. It was an incredible day, so beautiful and bright, Elaine had told the baby's mother she should name him Sunny. She laughed and told Elaine it was a beautiful name.

Elaine leafed through some more pictures, most of them from her childhood and adolescence. Seeing Campbell in so many of them punched her in the chest and made her shut the drawer.

She put her head in her hands for a few moments, trying to quiet everything that picked at her brain, making her head pound.

The journal was in the bottom left drawer, one of the last places Elaine looked. As soon as she picked up the aged and weathered journal, she was a child again. Although she knew the stories by heart, she never got tired of looking at her mom's family tree, of hearing the stories of her mom's family that had been passed down.

The weathered book sighed when she opened it, and several pieces of paper fluttered to the floor. Her hands trembled as she picked them up and unfolded them. She told herself to look away, but she couldn't peel her eyes from the letter that started with, *Dear Rain…*

I hope that by the time you read this letter we'll have had many wonderful conversations—some weekends together here or in New York, curled up on a couch with a bottle of wine, talking about everything and nothing. If you're reading this, and that hasn't happened, that's on me, and I can't tell you how sorry I am about it. I keep hoping you'll be able to forgive me someday. I don't ever want to push myself on you until you're ready.

I hope that one day you'll accept my invitations to come home for Christmas or Thanksgiving, but that hasn't happened yet. What

I wouldn't give to have you come home. I wish I could see the future, to see if it happens. I'm here whenever you're ready.

No matter what things are like between us when you read this, please know how proud I am of you. You were always so talented and smart. A hell of a lot smarter than me. God knows I didn't want you to go to New York. It terrified me and it hurt me too that you didn't want to stay, that you didn't like it here anymore. Even though I wish you weren't so far away, I'm proud of you for following your heart. You're doing things I could never dream of doing.

Every time I think of you, I smile. I see your red hair blowing in the wind, I see that beautiful, free spirit of yours that no one could crush. You are, and always have been my greatest joy, my greatest love.

I don't have much to leave you, but what I leave to you is precious. I'll trust you to do what's right with it.

She scanned the rest of the makeshift will, barely taking it in. She read enough to see that her mom's house, acreage, and animals would all go to her.

She let the journal drop to the floor. She didn't want it or the house or the land or the animals.

She just wanted her mom.

Violent waves of grief churned and roiled inside her. She got up and ran for the back door that led to the garden. Rain poured down on her, soaking her as she heaved—throwing up the remnants of wine and what little she'd eaten.

Words from the letter fell on her, pelting her like the rain.

What I wouldn't give to have you come home.

I'm here whenever you're ready.

Now Elaine saw what her mom meant when she said, "You're not my daughter." It wasn't a denouncement; it was her way of saying she didn't recognize who Elaine was anymore. It was a statement full of grief and confusion, not anger and abandonment.

Now she saw what every letter and every phone call she'd gotten on holidays and birthdays meant. She'd thought her mom only contacted her out of obligation, but now she realized it was her mom's way of reaching out to her, telling her she'd missed her, that she loved her.

"Why didn't you just say it?!" she screamed at the sky.

A rumble of thunder answered her.

"Why didn't you just tell me you missed me, that you were sorry?"

The answer made her retch again. Elaine remembered how busy she'd been every time her mom called, never staying on the phone long enough to have a real conversation. Now, she realized they both wanted the same thing. They both wanted to find their way back to each other.

Now it was too late.

"I'm sorry, Mom!" She pounded her fists into the muddy earth. "I'm so sorry," she sobbed, choking on her tears and the water that splashed up from the ground. "Can you even hear me? Oh, god, please tell me you can hear me!"

She curled up and lay on the ground, the rain and mud soaking through her clothes. She pulled her knees to her chest and lay there, sobbing, begging for forgiveness, begging for her mom to hear her.

The cold early morning air and the rain soaked through every pore, making her shiver. She closed her eyes and gave herself to the earth, to the torrent that poured over her, to the coldness that consumed her from inside and out.

When the first hint of dawn colored the sky orange, the rain stopped. Elaine looked at herself, her clothes, her hair, her skin covered in cold mud. She stripped her clothes off in the yard and walked back into the house naked, numb, and cold.

Her body and mind were numb as she heated water and took a bath. The warmth brought her back to the moment, made her feel just a little something. Something she couldn't place yet.

Since all of her clothes were back at the hotel, Elaine went to her mom's room to get something to wear. She smiled when she saw her mom's favorite sundress. The bright yellow was faded, but it was still pretty. Elaine slipped it on and grabbed a sweater to wear over it.

It was the first time in years that she felt close to her mom again.

She slipped on her mom's mud boots and did the morning chores in a peaceful kind of silence, then stayed outside and worked in the garden. There was a beautiful simplicity when she tended the garden, her hands connecting with the earth, with life. There was an immediacy, a sense of mindfulness that came with caring for the land and animals. It was the kind of calm purpose that had been missing from her life since she'd moved away.

With each minute and hour that ticked away, Elaine connected more to the earth, to the little farm, to her mom. To herself.

It wasn't until she came back inside for something to eat that she remembered the broken wine bottle. While she swept up the glass, she thought about Campbell, about last night, about the way he left. How had everything gone so wrong between them?

Campbell's words came back to her. *Memories are strange things.*

They'd begun to drift apart their sophomore year. Partway through her junior year, their friendship died.

High school had been her awakening. During elementary and middle school, she and Campbell went to a small rural school, but they went to high school in the middle of Durango along with a thousand other students. It didn't take her long to want a different kind of life, a normal kind of life that most of the other kids had.

By their junior year, Elaine had a new group of friends who went to football and basketball games, who lived in the 21st century and had everything she wanted but didn't have. She and Campbell still talked sometimes outside of school, but not during school, until the day he found out she was dating a guy from the basketball team.

He caught her in the commons. "What are you doing?" he asked.

"What do you mean?"

"That guy, Brett. What are you doing with him?"

His harsh tone put her on the defensive. "He's my boyfriend."

"He's about as smart as your mom's goat." He shook his head. "I take that back, it's an insult to the goat."

She glared at him. "You've never even talked to him, so don't get all judgey."

"I know enough. I hear him talk, especially about his girlfriends." He lowered his voice and looked at her with concern. "You're gonna get hurt."

She thought about the past week since they'd been dating, how Brett doted on her, couldn't get enough of her. "You don't know him," she hissed, "so stay out of it."

He let out a sigh. "I guess I don't know you either. Not anymore."

She rolled her eyes. "You sound like my mom."

She jumped when she felt someone come up behind her and put their arms around her waist. "Hey, Rainy." It was Brett.

Campbell gave her a disgusted look. "I've gotta go."

She felt a little bad as she watched him walk away.

"Who's that?" Brett asked.

"Nobody."

"He looks like a nobody," Brett chuckled.

"He is."

Campbell stopped and turned around, giving her one last look. She didn't understand the look on his face then. She didn't understand it until now because she hadn't thought about it in such a long time. Now, sitting in the sunny kitchen, it hit her with a sickening thud.

He'd heard everything she and Brett said. Campbell had heard her say he was a nobody—the person who'd been her best friend, the person who knew all her secrets and all her dreams. He'd held onto hers, and she'd held onto his.

Feeling sick with the memory, Elaine went outside to sit on the front steps, letting the sun wash over her. She wished it would cleanse her and take away all the awful things she'd done to the people she loved the most.

How had she gotten so lost? She thought she'd found herself in New York, thought she'd found her purpose through her work. She'd been so set on proving she was more, that her life was somehow better than the one her mom lived. It blinded her to the things, the people who mattered the most.

She ran inside the house and grabbed her phone. The battery was down to five percent and she prayed it would last long enough to send the text.

I'm sorry about last night. Can we please talk? My phone's about dead, but could you meet me at the river when you're done with work today? I'll wait there for you. Please come.

Elaine spent the rest of the day gathering things to take to the river. She found her old camping backpack and packed some food and water. The sleeping bags and tent were still in the closet like they'd always been. Regardless of whether

Campbell showed up, she wanted to camp at the river, needing to feel that connection to the land and to nature again.

##

It was after five when she made the mile trek through the pasture to the little river. She still wore the sundress and sweater along with a pair of her mom's lightweight hiking boots.

The landscape called to her, making her pay attention to every detail—to the hawk who glided by looking for prey, to the wind that swept in from the mountains, to the pines whose branches sang and bowed in the wind. She sucked in a breath of mountain air as if she were breathing in pieces of herself.

When she reached her spot by the little river, time hadn't changed it much. The banks had eroded a bit more, but all the landmarks were still there. When she saw the remnants of the fort she and Campbell had built so many years ago, she stopped and clutched her chest. Memories clawed at her heart—joy and innocence mixed with regret and longing. Everything she'd had and everything she'd lost was there in the rotting wood of the little lean-to where she'd spent so much of her life. Even after she'd lost Campbell, she'd come here when she needed it, like when Brett ended up breaking her heart, or anytime she needed an escape.

By the time she pitched the tent and unpacked some of her things, the sun began to set behind the foothills and mountains to the west. She put a sleeping bag in front of the tent and sat on it, then wrapped a blanket around her shoulders. The ache in her chest expanded every time the sun sank a little lower. As much as she'd hoped to see him, it looked like Campbell wasn't coming. He must have thought there was too much damage to repair. If only it were as easy as fixing the little dams they used to build in the river.

Elaine got up and walked to the riverbank, needing a distraction. It was only a few yards wide and was never more than knee deep during the summer. In spring when the snow melted, the little river raged for a time, sometimes swelling over the banks. But now, in late June, it settled into a mellow rhythm.

She slipped off the hiking boots and socks, then stepped down the bank and into the water. The icy water woke her up and made her forget her grief for a few moments as she walked up the river.

When she turned around to walk the river back to where she'd left her shoes, she saw his silhouette. His long legs ate up the ground as he walked toward her.

Her heart no longer hurt. It flew from her body, pulling her forward, making her clamor up the riverbank. She didn't waste time putting on her socks and shoes, instead, she ran to him, barely noticing the rough ground. As soon as she reached him, she wrapped her arms around him.

"I'm so glad you came," she whispered.

He stood there in silence, just stood there stiff, as if her joy at seeing him didn't matter. Although her arms were around him, his silence created a fissure between them.

She held him tighter, willing him to feel something, anything, even if it was anger. "Campbell?"

He put one arm around her, hesitant at first. As soon as his hand touched the small of her back, something inside of him seemed to shift. He gathered her in his arms, pulling her close as he let out a sigh.

If this was all there ever was between them, she'd take it. If this was the last time she'd see him, the last memory of him, she'd hold onto it as tightly as she held onto him.

He pulled back and ran his fingers over her frizzy curls and grinned at her. "You look like you again."

She took his hand. "I feel like me." She tilted her head and looked at his chestnut eyes. "You've always been you, haven't you."

The curious look he gave her carried a hint of sadness, making her wonder what he'd been through. "I don't know who else to be." He looked over and nodded at her tent. "I didn't know you were making camp here."

"Yeah, I missed it. I didn't know how much until today. You, um, you want something to eat or drink?"

He shook his head, but followed her to the tent where they sat on the sleeping bag outside. She pulled the sweater closer around her, trying to stave off the cool evening air.

"So, you're trying to get your fill of this before you go back to New York?"

She couldn't blame him for sounding wary. All she'd talked about since she'd gotten there was heading back to New York. She tried to read his eyes as dusk crept over the meadow. "How can people be so sure about their lives? About who they are and what they want? How did you know?"

His laughter was flavored with bitterness. "You don't think I've ever been confused? Lost? Fuck, I'm about as lost as—I don't know what. But just because my life might look simple, it doesn't mean it's easy."

Her cheeks burned. "That's not what I meant." She was about to defend herself but stopped. "I'd like to hear about your life if—if you want to tell me. I'm still your friend."

The look he gave her was as cold as last night's rain. "Are you? Because friends don't just walk away. Friends don't stay away for years without a word."

She hardened against his words. "It goes two ways, Campbell. You could have reached out too." She took a breath, trying to steady herself. "You don't think I missed you? That I needed you?"

He leaned forward and rested his elbows on his knees. "No, you made it pretty clear what was important and what wasn't. You changed your name for god's sake. Were you really that ashamed of your life?" The words he didn't speak screamed at her, the silent ones assuming that she was ashamed of him.

"No, I was never—" She pictured his face after she'd said he was a nobody. For the first time, she saw the truth. "You're right," she sighed. "I'm sorry. I'm so sorry about how awful I was to my mom and to you." She fought the tears that stung her eyes. "I feel selfish even asking for a second chance." She put her hand on his shoulder, hoping he wouldn't shrug it away, hoping he'd finally look at her. "I already lost one of the most important people in my life. I don't want to lose the other one."

He did look at her, but it was too dark to read his eyes. "What do you want?" he asked, still sounding wary.

She moved her hand from his shoulder and placed it over his hand. "What do I want?" she asked, her voice shaking.

"Yes, what do you want?" His voice was thick with emotion.

"To talk, to know you again, to hear about your life."

He nodded and looked at the ground, making her wonder if he was about to get up and walk away. "You really want to know?"

She squeezed his hand. "I do."

He filled in the lost years, telling her how he'd built his business, how he helped her mom farm and garden and grow her own business. And he told her about Anna, his fiancé. There was a lightness to his voice when he talked about meeting her and how they connected, how they seemed so right for each other. Eventually, his tone grew heavier when he talked about how it fell apart after two years together—too many arguments about how much time he spent working, too many arguments about what their lives should look like.

"I know relationships aren't easy," he said, "but it got to the point where we made each other unhappy a lot more than we made each other happy."

"I'm really sorry, Campbell."

"Yeah, me too, but I don't think either of us was ready. We were both pretty young." He turned to face her. "What about you? Is there someone in New York?"

She shook her head. "I dated some, but it was just…weird. It was hard for me to find someone to relate to, someone who didn't laugh at me and make Little House on the Prairie jokes when I told them about my childhood."

He chuckled at her. "Do you like it there? Does it feel like home?"

Home. The mountain air swirled around her and carried her away. *Welcome home.* She was surrounded by family in a mountain meadow, holding her mom's hand, thousands of people joined together. *Welcome home. Lovin' you.*

"No, it's not home," she whispered. "I love my work—what I do. I love creating something out of nothing, but New York's not home."

"What do you want?" he asked again.

His question stirred something inside of her, swelling in her chest, big and beautiful like the mountain's around them. She glanced at the first stars lighting the evening sky. In one long, deep breath, she breathed it all in, seeing the truth that surrounded her. Seeing the truth right in front of her.

She traced Campbell's jawline with her finger, drawing his attention to her. She hoped he could read what she wanted in her touch.

"Elaine," he said with a hint of warning.

She pulled back, embarrassed. "I'm sorry. I thought—well, I thought you felt something too. But if you don't want that, it's okay. Just tell me what you want." She looked down, trying to hide the sting of rejection.

His hand under her chin made her look up.

"What do I want?" he asked, like he was asking the universe. "I want something that's crazy, that makes no sense." He pulled his hand away.

"Come to the Rainbow Gathering with me," she said. The idea flew from her mouth, but as crazy as it sounded, it felt right.

"What?" He sounded just as surprised as she was.

"Come to the gathering with me."

"I thought you needed to get back to New York."

She shook her head. "I think I need some time away to figure things out."

"Can you do that? Can you get time away?"

She looked at the faint outline of the San Juans, wondering if she could really go back to her life in a land of concrete and noise. "I should be able to. I can count on one hand how many days I've taken off in the six years I've worked there." She glanced at his hands that were back in his lap. "Can you take time off?"

He shrugged. "I'd have to rearrange some things, push back a few projects. Most of my clients are pretty laid back."

"So will you go?" she asked.

"Why?"

There was no easy answer, but she'd try. "Because you'd love it. There's nothing like it—being with thousands of strangers who become family. When someone welcomes you home, or says, 'Lovin' you,' they mean it. When you help out in one of the kitchens or gather firewood, you know you're a part of something bigger than yourself." She sighed and looked at her hands that had grown soft and delicate over the last decade. "And it's a place where you can't run away from yourself. Not that you need it, but I need to be somewhere like that, where I have to face who I am."

He let out a breath like he'd been holding it in. "And who are you?"

"I don't know." She glanced at their old fort. "I'm the girl who lived for the summers she spent here with you. I'm the girl who loved to build things, create things, who wasn't afraid to get her hands dirty. But…" Her voice got softer. "But I'm also the person who ran away from all of that. I thought I was running to something better, but now…"

"Now what?"

"Now I have so many regrets, things I can't fix." Her stomach twisted with those regrets. "There's so much I wish I could take back, so much wasted time."

"You're not the only one with regrets."

His comment caught her off guard. "What do you mean?"

"Your mom always knew where you were. I could have—"

"I could have too." She remembered how lonely she was when she first moved to New York. She never knew she could feel that alone among millions of people. There were so many times she wanted to talk to him, to hear his voice.

He leaned back and looked at the sky. "All that regret—it doesn't change a damn thing."

He was right, but he was also wrong. She moved closer and turned to face him. "It can stop us from making the same mistakes again," she whispered, leaning toward him.

He leaned forward, searching her eyes. "Elaine?" There were so many questions within her name, but the sound of it coming from Campbell didn't feel right.

"Call me Rain." She said it to him and the river and the mountains and the night. They listened and welcomed her name, absorbed it, and gave it back to her. "Call me Rain." She needed to hear it again.

He got on his knees and took her face in his hands. "I've missed you so much."

She could only nod. Words would never be enough, so she kissed him, hoping her lips, her body would tell him how much she missed him, how much she cared about him.

They kissed until her lips felt swollen and her body pulsed with a need to be even closer. They lay down on the sleeping bag.

"Should we go inside the tent?" he asked, sounding as breathless as she felt.

"No." She needed to see the stars and the moon and the indigo sky.

She reached for the light wool blanket she'd tossed aside earlier. Campbell pulled it over them, then leaned down to kiss her. She pulled off his sweatshirt and T-shirt and ran her hands down his chest, making him suck in a breath. Not wanting anything between them, she wriggled out of the sweater and began to pull at the straps of her dress when Campbell stopped her.

"Let me," he whispered.

His fingers touched the straps and gently pulled them down over her shoulders. When he pulled the dress down, she closed her eyes, longing for his fingers, his lips to be where the night air met her skin.

"You're beautiful," he sighed. Then he touched her, making goosebumps erupt on her skin while the rest of her burned.

Their breath met in a frosty collision, the sound of it becoming louder than the river as they shed the rest of their clothes. She felt his need just as strong as her own when their bodies joined.

They lay together afterwards, their bodies close, trying to insulate themselves from the cold. The river played a gentle melody, soothing her, making her sleepy.

"Campbell?"

"Yeah?"

There was so much she wanted to say. Hopefully they'd have enough time together for her to say those things, for the two of them to know each other again.

"Does this mean you'll go to the Rainbow Gathering with me? Even if you've never been there before, it's like going home."

He kissed her and pulled her even closer. "Yeah, I'll go to the gathering."

HEY BROTHER

Tuesday, June 30

If Talon was going to have one more night of freedom, tonight was the night. His parents would never suspect that he'd sneak out in the torrential rainstorm. He'd taken to spending most of his time in his room, so his parents barely acknowledged him. He had no access to his phone or computer, so they figured he'd be free from sin until tomorrow when they'd send him away.

The rain pounded against his window, making a tinny noise like a snare drum. The drop from the upstairs balcony would be trickier in the rain, but when it was dry, he could make the escape in his sleep.

Escape. He'd almost made it. His eighteenth birthday was only a month and a half away. If he could have made it until then, he would have been free, and no one could force him into a program like LIGHT. It was some bullshit acronym about Living In God's Holy Truth.

Talon slipped his lightweight raincoat on—the expensive jacket made of the best waterproof material. His parents bought it along with the best sleeping bag and tent money could buy. Heading off into the woods for a week was part of LIGHT's monthlong program. He'd read that they kept some people longer, but once he was eighteen, no one could force him to be there.

He stepped out of the window of his third story bedroom and made his way to the edge of the roof. It was so dark there was no ground below, just a swirling abyss of water and the inky black night. He inched closer to the edge and closed his eyes. He could do it, he could dive head first off the roof, break his neck, and it would be over. It wasn't the first time he'd thought about it.

"Talon?"

The sound of Delphine's voice almost made him fall. He inched back from the edge to where she stood at his window.

"What are you doing?" The sound of fear in Delphine's voice made him feel bad. She was the only one of his four siblings who didn't treat him like a leper. At ten she was probably too young to get it, but she was different too—more open, more sensitive.

"I'm just going out for a walk," he said, trying to sound casual.

"In the rain?"

He leaned down and ruffled her long black hair. "Yeah, you like to play in the rain, don't you?"

Her grin made her eyes sparkle. "Can I come?"

"It's too late, and I don't want you to get in trouble."

All traces of her smile disappeared into the night. "You're in trouble, aren't you. It's why you're going away tomorrow."

He swallowed against the fear rising in his chest. "Yeah, but I won't be gone for long."

"Promise?"

What if he didn't come back soon? What if LIGHT could somehow force him to stay even after he turned eighteen?

He gave her a nod, but he couldn't say the promise out loud in case it wasn't true. "I'll write to you. How does that sound?"

"Okay, and I'll write back." She looked at him, her eyes fierce. "I won't tell Mom and Dad you snuck out tonight."

He knelt down and tickled her ribs. "Have I told you you're the best little sister in the whole world?"

"All the time," she giggled, the sound of it warming him against the cold rain.

"I'll see you in the morning."

"See you," she said, and shut the window. A second later, the light in his room went out and he was alone in the darkness again.

This time, he didn't think about jumping. It would kill Delphine to see him like that. If he was going to do it, he'd do it while he was at LIGHT.

It didn't take Talon long to shimmy down the roof and quietly drop to the second story balcony. Then he stepped over the rail, grabbed it, and let his body hang down. The drop was far enough to break an ankle or leg if you landed wrong, but Talon landed light on his feet like he always did. Then he snuck around the side of the house, knowing exactly how to avoid the motion sensors.

He took a quick look over his shoulder at what he called their "ranchion." It was much too big to be called a ranch house.

It was more like a small mansion set on one hundred acres of prime land just outside of Heber, Utah.

He found his mountain bike halfway down their lane where he always kept it hidden in the middle of a grove of pines. He'd told his parents it had been stolen.

He got on and rode into the darkness, into the rain.

##

It took Talon thirty minutes to bike into town. By that time, his hands were practically frozen to the handlebars and his teeth chattered against the cold mountain night. He went straight to one of the gas stations in town to buy the hottest cup of coffee he could get. As he biked toward the door, he was met by shouting.

"If you're not gonna buy anything, you can't be here!" Luke Everett yelled at five people standing beneath the store awning. Luke was in Talon's graduating class and had perfected his role as a bully.

The people Luke yelled at looked just as cold and wet as Talon, minus the good jacket. A couple of the guys had dreadlocks and most of their clothes were worn. They were probably headed to the Rainbow Gathering up in the mountains just outside of Heber. It officially started tomorrow, but Talon had seen people traveling there all month. The last few days it seemed like hundreds or even thousands came through.

It was all over the news, how ten to twenty thousand people would come through Heber on their way to the gathering. There was a lot of tension surrounding it. Business owners and residents—including his dad—were worried about thieves and violence and vagrants, despite assurances that most people who went to gatherings were peaceful and didn't cause trouble.

Talon walked up to Luke. "Chill out," he said in a soft voice. He and Luke weren't friends, but Talon was never one of Luke's targets. "In case you haven't noticed, there's more of them than you. Besides, they're just hanging out." Talon was fascinated by all the people he'd seen come through town. It was a nice change to see people who looked a little different than the general population of Heber. Whenever he could get away from his house, he'd bike into town or up to the forest service road and watch the people headed to the gathering. Sometimes people stopped to talk to him. Most of them seemed friendly enough.

Luke puffed up his chest. "They were out here begging, bugging the customers, scaring them away. My manager says no loitering."

One of the young women in the group laughed. "Yeah, we're pretty scary looking."

"And we're not begging," a guy said, his face hidden beneath a hooded sweatshirt.

Something about the vulnerability in his voice caught Talon's attention. He squinted, trying to catch a glimpse of the guy's face beneath his hood, but couldn't.

"But if someone offered to buy us something to eat or drink, we wouldn't turn it down," a guy with dreadlocks said.

Luke narrowed his eyes and balled his hands into fists. "I'm gonna go in and call the cops, so you better fucking scatter. NOW!"

Talon's heart leapt into his throat. Most of the cops were friends with his dad. The sheriff was a good friend. Talon was in enough trouble without word getting back to his dad that he was in town tonight.

"Hold on," Talon hissed. "You don't need to call the cops." He nodded toward the store. "Come on."

"What are you doing?" Luke demanded when they got inside.

"Ring up five slices of pizza, five large sodas, and one coffee," Talon said.

"What? What are you doing? You're not feeding them. It'll just encourage them."

The heat in Talon's cheeks spread and took away the chill from the rain. "Fuck, they're not animals. Besides, are you gonna turn away paying customers? I doubt your manager would want to hear that you turned down money."

Luke glared at Talon, but he walked behind the register to ring up the pizza and drinks.

Talon paid, then grabbed his coffee and walked outside to the group of people. "You guys can go in and grab a slice of pizza and some soda if you want to. It's on me."

"Seriously?" one of the girls said.

Talon grinned at her. "Yeah."

Everybody nodded at Talon or thanked him. The girl bringing up the rear stopped and hugged him. "Blessings," she said to him. Seeing her up close, she couldn't have been more than sixteen. It made him wonder about her life, if she had a family who cared about her or was worried about her.

Talon biked away from the gas station and headed to one of the town parks. It was one of his favorite places to go at night, especially when it was deserted like it was now. He went to one of the small shelters to escape the rain and sat on top of a picnic table where he shook the excess water from his black hair.

He held the coffee to warm his hands and breathed in his last night of freedom. He thought about getting on his bike and riding as far as he could. But where? He couldn't get far without any money that was truly his. His bank account was tied into his dad's account, so his dad could close it or take all the money out at any time.

"It's just a month," he whispered to the night air, his words carried away, absorbed by the mist and the rain. He could survive a month. His lungs tightened, making it hard to breathe. But a month could be a long time, especially if there were people at LIGHT who'd try to break him.

Laughter from across the street made Talon look up. It was the group of people from the gas station. He hoped they'd given Luke a hard time—not enough for the police to be called, but enough to mess with Luke. The asshole had it coming.

As he watched them round the corner, he longed for what they had—friendship, people you could count on, people you could laugh with, people who knew you, who accepted you.

No one in Heber knew him. He'd grown up here. Everyone thought he had a lot of friends. Everyone thought he had it made, that he was a golden child.

No one knew him.

Two weeks ago, when his parents checked his computer and caught a glimpse of who he really was, it was painfully clear just how repulsed they were by him, by the one thing that made up so much of who he was. It was so awful, so shameful, they were sending him away in a hush of secrecy in the hopes of changing him. They couldn't ruin their image, their status of being the perfect family, the one every other family in Heber, Utah wanted to be.

He leaned forward and put his head in his hands, wishing things were different, wishing he'd been born like everyone else in his family. Life would have been so much easier. Instead, his whole life was a lie—pretending to ogle girls with his friends, dating the girls his family approved of. He'd kissed those girls, made out with them, but felt nothing, unless he closed his eyes and imagined they were Ellis Markham, the beautiful, soft-spoken guy who was into art. Ellis was the only openly gay student in high school and was brutally harassed every day by people like Luke.

"You okay?"

The voice made Talon jump. He looked up to see the guy in the hooded sweatshirt standing in front of him.

Talon ran a hand through his hair. "You scared the shit out of me."

"Sorry," the guy said. He pulled off his hood to reveal shaggy, sandy brown hair. "I just wanted to say thanks for the pizza and stuff. Most people aren't that nice."

"No problem. Luke can be a real asshole. I hope you gave him a hard time."

The guy shook his head. "We didn't want any trouble. Just wanted to get out of the rain."

"Sorry about that. Not everybody in Heber is an asshole." He grinned. "Just seventy percent of them."

The guy laughed. "I'm River."

"Is that your real name?" Talon shook his head, telling himself to shut up. "I didn't mean—"

"No worries. It's my rainbow name, but it's what I go by most of the time now."

"I'm Talon," he said and stuck his hand out.

River took it and held it for a few moments, then smiled. "Is that your real name?"

Talon laughed, the first real laugh in weeks. "Yeah. I think my mom prided herself in giving all of us kind of unusual names.

River sat beside Talon and wrapped his arms around himself like he was trying to get warm. "I like it."

"So you're headed to the Rainbow Gathering?" *Idiot. Of course he's going there. He just told you his rainbow name.*

"Yeah, a group of us are going. What about you?"

Talon turned toward River, trying to get a better look at him in the dim glow of a nearby streetlight. There was a warmth and a spark in his brown eyes that made Talon want to study them, study him. Finally, he pulled his eyes away, hoping he hadn't been too obvious.

"No, I just live here. Besides, I'm, well, I'm getting sent—I mean, I'm going away for a while. Leaving tomorrow."

"That sucks. You might like the gathering."

He chanced another look at River's eyes, hoping he wasn't imagining the curiosity, the intensity mirrored back at him. "I think I would," he said in a soft voice.

River rubbed his arms and his teeth began to chatter. "Fuck, it's freezing here," he said. "We heard it would be even colder in the mountains."

"It's freezing up there at night. I hope you brought some warm clothes."

"I'll manage, I always do," he said through chattering teeth.

Talon looked down at the picnic table. "I, um, I've got a sweatshirt under my jacket. It's dry if you want to put it on—get warmed up, at least for now."

"Man, that would be great." He peeled off his soaked sweatshirt and T-shirt, revealing lean muscles in his stomach and arms.

Talon took off his jacket and sweatshirt, handed the sweatshirt to River, and put his jacket back on. It was hard not to stare at River—at his tall, lanky body, his messy hair, his gorgeous eyes.

"Thanks, man."

Talon shrugged, feeling embarrassed.

"My group's camped about a mile outside of town if you want to come and hang out with us. There's about fifteen of us now. We don't have a lot, but we'll share what we have."

He wanted to say yes. A fantasy unfolded where he'd go with River and be accepted into his group. They'd offer to let Talon join them, to travel with them. Then he could just disappear, fall off his parents' radar. Then there'd be no conversion program in Salt Lake City, no more life where he'd be forced to be someone he wasn't. But it wasn't that simple. His dad had plenty of resources to find Talon. If his dad found him with River's group, his dad would most likely press charges, especially if Talon was still a minor.

"That sounds great, but I—I can't."

River looked down and nodded. "I just thought, well, I guess I thought wrong."

Talon's heart raced. The force of it surged through his body until he felt it beat in his fingertips and echo in his ears. "Did you follow me here?" Talon asked. The adrenaline stole his voice, making it barely a whisper.

River still wouldn't look at him. "Yeah, but it was just to say thanks and to—sorry, I was—"

Talon put his hand on River's shoulder and scooted closer. He never imagined he'd be this bold, but he had nothing left to lose at this point.

River looked up, his eyes wide.

"You weren't wrong," Talon said.

The words were barely out of his mouth when River kissed him. Urgent kisses, like his lips and tongue were starved. Talon sighed and his breath grew ragged as each kiss fueled the heat that pulsed through his veins. This was what he always imagined kissing would be like. No, it was better than anything he imagined. Everything was magnified—the rain drumming on the shelter roof, the pounding rhythm matching his wild heartbeat. River held Talon's face in his hands while Talon's hands shook, but not from the cold.

River pulled Talon closer until Talon swore he felt the beat of River's heart against his. They scrambled to get even closer, and Talon let out a groan as he grew hard against River's body.

The rain, the mist, the cold all swirled around them, but couldn't touch them. It created a barrier that felt like a shield from the rest of the world. He wanted to lay naked in the grass, to live out every fantasy he'd had, to screw and fuck and make love—whatever they wanted to call it.

River put his hand on Talon's knee and slid it up to his thigh.

"Don't stop," Talon breathed into his ear.

Then River's hand was on his erection, rubbing it through his jeans.

It felt like a dream when River lifted Talon's jacket and T-shirt to kiss his chest, his stomach. "You're gorgeous," River whispered. He undid the button and zipper on Talon's jeans.

It all felt so good, too good.

A blast from a car horn down the street broke through the veiled fantasy, making Talon remember that he was still in small town Heber, Utah. A place where it wasn't a good idea to make out with another guy out in the open, especially for Talon. "Wait," he said, breathless.

"What's wrong?" River asked.

"Someone's gonna see us."

River kissed him. "No one's going to be out walking in the rain." He kissed Talon's neck and touched his thigh again.

"You were," Talon sighed.

"I was looking for you."

"We should go somewhere more private. People here aren't used to seeing this."

"I don't care," River said. He moved his hand up higher, making it hard for Talon to think.

"I wish I didn't," Talon said, pulling away. He reached down to zip and button his jeans.

River leaned forward and rested his elbows on his knees. "You're not out, are you."

Talon shook his head, embarrassed. "If you had my family, my life, you wouldn't be out either." He absentmindedly played with the zipper on his jacket. "I was gonna tell my parents, but not until I moved away. But they snooped around on my computer and found stuff no straight guy wouldn't be watching."

River looked more closely at him. "How old are you?"

"I just graduated, but I'm not eighteen for another month and a half."

River let out a breath that sounded like relief. "You had me worried for a minute that you were fifteen or something. You don't look like it, but…"

"And how old are you?"

"Almost nineteen," River said. "You know, you could leave home now, come with us. A lot of us left before we were eighteen."

Talon balled his fist in frustration. "It's not that easy. I'm going to college this fall, that's when I was going to tell them. The worst they could do then was cut me off, force me to make my own way in life. I can handle that."

River shook his head, looking confused. "And what can they do to you now that's so terrible?"

Talon ran a hand down his face, trying to gather himself. "They're sending me to a conversion program tomorrow."

"A what?"

"You know—pray the gay away. People there tell you you're sick, that you just need to find God. Who knows what else they'll do. It's some private facility that's supposed to have a great success rate." His voice began to shake. "Fuck…fuck me."

River grabbed his hand. "Don't go."

"I don't have a choice."

"Yes you do," River said, sounding frustrated. "Come with us and disappear into the gathering."

Talon shook his head. "You don't know my dad. He's mega rich and he has everyone in his back pocket, including the cops. And I'm still a minor. If they found me with you, they could arrest all of you for kidnapping."

"They're not gonna find us. There'll be at least ten thousand people at the gathering. There'll be some law enforcement, but you can usually stay hidden from them." He squeezed Talon's hand. "Come on, we'll get you to the gathering. You can either hang with us or go your own way. But I hope—"

Talon leaned over and kissed him, the memories of what happened earlier still coursed through him. "This is crazy," he said. In the back of his mind he wondered what River would think if he found out Talon had never been with a guy before. He'd have to tell him at some point, but he was too chicken to do it now.

River grinned at him. "Crazy is good. People always tell me I need to be a little crazier, so let's be crazy together." He pulled Talon close like he did before. "We'll find a more private spot once we get to our campsite," he whispered in Talon's ear. Then he kissed him.

Talon kissed him back, wishing they could be together right there on the picnic table. A car horn beeped again, but this one was much closer, the beep stretching out long and loud.

Fear replaced the fire in his body.

"Talon!" His dad's voice made his heart freeze.

Why couldn't anyone else have found him? Anyone. "Dammit! Fuck, fuck, fuck!"

River grabbed Talon's hand and tugged on it. "Come on."

"I can't. That's my dad. There's no way he's gonna let me walk away."

River shook his head in confusion. "What's he gonna do?"

Talon hung his head. "You don't know my dad."

"Talon!" His dad called again through the open car window. "Get over here. Now!"

Talon started to stand, but River tightened his grip on Talon's hand. "We're camped just a little ways up the forest service road," River said. "There's a couple of old busses. A rainbow one and a dark blue one. Come and find us if you can get away."

Talon's stomach rolled, making him nauseous. "They won't let me out of their sight now. But just in case, hide my bike in those trees on the far side of the park and I'll try to find you."

"If you look for us at our camp and we're gone, come to the gathering and look for the dirty kids. I don't know if I'll stay with them, but they'll know where I'm at."

"Dirty kids? Who are they?"

"It's just a name some of us go by." River grabbed him and kissed him one more time. Talon blocked out his dad until he heard a car door slam shut. When he saw his dad walking toward them, he pulled away.

"I have to go," Talon whispered.

"Get away if you can." River squeezed his hand. "Don't let them change you."

He wanted to say he wouldn't, but he honestly didn't know what would happen.

"Wait," River said, "your sweatshirt."

"Keep it."

River grabbed his soaked hoodie from the picnic table and tossed it to Talon. "We can give them back to each other at the gathering."

Talon balled up the hoodie and jogged toward his dad.

Talon's dad was quiet during the drive home. His dad was never quiet. Talon would have been less scared if his dad screamed at him during the drive home. Every silent minute that passed felt more charged, more dangerous. Talon slumped down in the front seat, wishing he could disappear.

When they got home and walked into the house, Talon's mom was sitting in the living room. She sat with her hands in her lap, her fingers fidgeting while she glanced from Talon to his dad. She opened her mouth, then closed it and looked at the floor.

"Go to your room," his dad ordered. His voice was barely contained.

Talon went upstairs, shed his jacket and T-shirt, then lay face down on his bed, trying not to think about his parents and what they were talking about. It didn't matter. They couldn't do anything worse to him than send him to LIGHT, could they?

He let the sound of the rain carry him back through town and out to the forest service road where River waited for him. He held onto that image like a tether that would keep him from falling. From jumping.

It felt like at least twenty minutes passed by the time he heard his bedroom door open. He sat up as his dad walked in and closed the door behind him. The look his dad gave him was colder than the icy rain.

"How dare you." His voice was so calm, so controlled, it was terrifying. "How dare you flaunt your sin in front of everyone."

"It's—it's not—"

"Quiet! You don't get to talk right now!"

Talon pulled his knees to his chest, wishing he could hide.

"We've tried everything," his dad said. "We talked to you, took away your computer and phone, grounded you, made you go to church more, prayed for you. And none of it's worked." He paced across the floor. "I've been too easy on you, let too many things slide." His dad stopped and unbuckled his belt. "It's time you had the fear of God in you."

Talon sat frozen as he watched his dad free his belt from his pants. He'd gotten spanked as a kid. They'd all gotten spanked when they were younger—spanked with an open hand across their butts. It stung, but it usually didn't leave a mark.

"What are you doing?" Talon asked, his eyes glued to the belt in his dad's hands.

"You don't get to talk!" his dad barked again. "Get over here."

Talon slowly got up and stood face to face with his dad, trying not to show his fear.

"Turn around," his dad ordered.

"Dad…"

"Turn around!"

The first lash across his bare back stung so much, he fought not to cry out. He clenched his jaw and gritted his teeth against the next five lashes. When his dad didn't quit after five, Talon closed his eyes and tried to go away, tried to go back to the park in the rain to the most perfect moment in his life.

Finally, his dad stopped, his breath heavy like he'd just run for miles. "I didn't want to do that." Some of the coldness left his voice. "I just…I don't know what to do anymore. Hopefully the people at LIGHT will."

Talon wondered if the people at LIGHT would beat him too.

"You'll sleep in our room tonight, on the floor," his dad said. "That way we can keep track of you."

Talon stood with his back still to his dad. He couldn't face him, not right now. The feel of his dad's hand on his shoulder made him wince and pull away. "Talon, I'm…" his dad let out a deep sigh, but didn't finish his thought. Instead, he said, "Grab some blankets and pillows, come on."

Talon couldn't sleep. There was no way to get comfortable, even with a soft T-shirt covering his back. Every time he turned over, his back screamed in pain. He'd looked at it in the bathroom mirror, at angry welts that covered his back. It wasn't just the pain that kept him awake, it was LIGHT and it was River. LIGHT made him feel like his life was over while River gave him a glimpse of a beginning. A beginning that was over before it started.

After his parents were asleep, Talon found a notepad and pen on his mom's dresser. If he wrote about River, found some way to hide the paper and bring it with him, it might let him hold onto himself while he was at LIGHT. He'd heard the concept of a touchstone in one of his English classes. That's what the paper could be.

It was hard to see in the darkness of the bedroom, but Talon put his face close to the paper and wrote.

I remember kissing in the rain. The way he smelled, the way the water dripped from his hair and flavored his tongue when it

It was him and the rain that made me lose my mind, and made me forget about staying hidden. And I would do it again—I would take a hundred lashings to feel his hands on me, his heart beating against mine.

Talon had written before, had written out some of his fantasies, had even written some short stories—love stories between guys. He'd always destroyed them so there'd be no incriminating evidence, so no one would see the writer, the dreamer beneath the star athlete. But he wouldn't destroy what he'd just written unless someone found it and forced him to get rid of it.

He folded the piece of paper until it was tiny. Hopefully it was tiny enough to hide inside one of his socks or someplace in the clothing he'd pack. He assumed they'd search his things when he got to LIGHT, so he'd have to be careful about where he put it.

He pulled River's hoody from under his pillow. He'd hidden it in the blankets he'd brought to his parents' bedroom. The sweatshirt—the smell of River and cold rain and a hint of pot—was the only thing that brought Talon any comfort. He held it close, not caring that it was still damp.

##

Talon threw his suitcase in the trunk, then took his backpack and sunk into the back seat of his parents' luxury SUV. Although the day was going to be fairly warm, especially in Salt Lake City, he wore River's sweatshirt, needing something to give him strength and courage. He'd also snuck a small kitchen knife into the lining of his backpack in case things got too unbearable at LIGHT.

Talon winced when he put the seatbelt on, his back hurting even worse this morning. When his dad got in and started the car, Talon swallowed against the dread, against the feeling that his life was over. The way his parents acted didn't help. They'd barely spoken to him. His mom wouldn't even look at him.

By the time they reached Heber, Talon felt sick. He tried to tell himself he could survive a month at LIGHT, but he wasn't sure. He'd gotten onto his parents' computer a few days ago and researched conversion therapy and conversion centers after he'd heard them talk about it. Some of the stories he read were so terrifying, he'd gone to his mom and begged her not to send him. But she told him those stories about shock therapy and abuse were made up by the gay community. Talon wished he could believe that.

When they drove past the road that led to the park, full blown panic set in. "You have to stop," he said.

"Why?" His dad sounded suspicious.

"I'm gonna be sick." It wasn't a lie.

"You'll be fine."

His stomach lurched. Sweat dotted his forehead and trickled down his back. It was impossible to catch his breath. "I'm not fine!" he yelled, clutching his stomach. "I'm sick, I'm really sick."

His mom glanced back at him. "Robert, you need to stop," she said to his dad. "I don't want him getting sick in the car."

As soon as his dad pulled into a nearby gas station, Talon grabbed his backpack and got out.

"I'm coming with you," he heard his dad say behind him.

Talon couldn't wait. He ran for the bathroom at the back of the store and locked the door. He barely made it to the toilet in time to throw up what little he'd eaten for breakfast.

Afterward, he sat on the floor and leaned against the wall. His mind went to the knife in his backpack. He could do it here, just get it over with.

"Talon?" his dad called from outside the bathroom.

He coughed and made a gagging noise. "I'm still sick."

He grabbed his backpack and pulled out the knife, then touched the point against the soft skin on the inside of his wrist. If only there was a different way to escape. It wasn't like in the movies or TV. There was no window in the bathroom he could crawl out of and escape.

He looked at the knife in his hand. If he hadn't met River, if he hadn't felt all the possibilities in that kiss, he probably would have drug the blade down his forearm. But those brief moments with River whispered a promise to him, a promise of what things could be like once he got away from his parents, once he could have a life of his own. That promise made him put the knife back, but he didn't get up. He needed just a little more time to get himself together, to find the courage to go back to the car.

When Talon was finally ready, he cracked the bathroom door open to see where his dad was. Instead of being right outside the door, he was up at the register buying something. Talon's eyes flew to the back door of the gas station, knowing he might only have seconds to escape. He quietly shut the bathroom door behind him and glanced at his dad again. In that second, his dad turned around and saw him. Talon bolted out the back door, his dad's voice right behind him, yelling at him to stop.

He sprinted down alleys, behind businesses, and through yards, trying to stay off the main streets. Somewhere along the way, he lost his dad, but it wouldn't be long before his parents would drive around town, scouring every street until they found him. He thought about the park and his bike, but the park was too open, too visible. He needed someplace secluded where there'd be no people.

He ended up at the high school, which felt too obvious, but any hiding place he thought of felt too obvious. It wasn't easy to hide in a town that his parents knew so well. His eyes went to one of the dumpsters in the back of the school. He walked over to it, lifted the lid, and wrinkled his nose at the stench of stale garbage embedded in the metal dumpster. It was empty aside from a few big black garbage bags filled with who knows what. With a sigh of resignation, he hoisted himself into the dumpster and closed the lid. Tiny fragments of light shone through the loose-fitting lid, which meant there'd at least be some air flow.

Talon had nothing with him to track the time. His parents still had his cell phone. The only thing that gave him a hint of time was the sun and its painfully slow movement across the sky.

After a few hours, Talon grew a little more used to the stench. It no longer made him gag. Thankfully the dumpster sat under an overhang, giving him some much needed shade from the summer sun. As it was, his T-shirt was still drenched under his armpits and down his back. At least the smell took away his appetite. All he had in his backpack was one granola bar and a bottle of water. Throughout the day, he forced himself to only take small sips of water, knowing he needed to save some. Eventually the heat and the boredom lulled him in and out of sleep.

##

When dusk finally hit, Talon ventured out of the dumpster, his body stiff and sore from being in there all day. Now that it was almost dark, Talon chanced going to the park in hopes of finding his bike. He cut through yards, staying off the streets as much as he could. There would be more of a police presence now with the Rainbow Gathering, so he had to be extra cautious.

His heart swelled and he said a silent thank you to River when he found his mountain bike stuffed inside the thick grove of trees.

Adrenaline fueled him as he made his way out of Heber toward the roads that led to the gathering. After he left Heber behind him, some of the fear and tension lifted. Still, every time he heard a car, he got off the road and into the shadows just in case it was his parents or the police. He'd never told his parents about his fascination with the gathering, so hopefully they'd have no idea he was headed there.

When he reached the spot where he thought River's group might have camped, disappointment washed over him. There were no busses, no people. He pulled over to rest and took a small drink of water. He'd just pulled the granola bar out when he thought he heard a girl crying nearby.

"Hello?" he called.

The crying stopped.

"I'm not gonna hurt you. Are you okay?"

"Yes," a girl's voice answered, then she sniffled.

"You can come out," he said.

A few seconds later, she emerged from the trees and walked toward him. In the scant light of the moon, he could tell that her long dark hair was tangled. Although she wore several layers of clothing, she still looked cold. She was thin, the kind of thin that made him think she'd probably gone hungry more than once. She couldn't have been much older than he was, making him wonder what her life was like.

"You want some?" he asked, breaking the granola bar in half. Although it was the only thing he had to eat, he didn't feel right keeping it to himself.

She took the granola bar from him, then backed away a few steps. Maybe it was because she was scared, or because he smelled like garbage.

"Thanks," she said as she picked at the bar, savoring each piece of it.

He nodded. "Are you sure you're all right? Most people who are crying aren't okay."

She sat on the ground. "I'm not hurt or anything. I just… I don't know what to do."

He sat across from her, but didn't get too close, giving her the space she seemed to need. "About what?"

"I was going to the gathering with my best friend and we— well, we met up with more people just outside of Utah and they gave us a ride. They were okay and everything, but then my friend, he got beat up last night—beat up real bad. Bad enough they had to take him to the hospital." She choked back a sob.

"I'm sorry," Talon said. It didn't surprise him, especially because of how some of the locals talked about the gathering. "Is he gonna be okay?"

"I think so." She wiped her nose on her coat sleeve. "They broke his arm and one of them had a knife, and, well they want to keep him in the hospital a few days. I was gonna stay with him, but he told me I should go to the gathering and he'd meet me there later. I should've stayed with him. Now I can't find the people we came with. They left without us."

"That sucks." He wished he could think of something better to say, something that would make her feel better. "You can, um, you can travel with me if you want to. I'm alone too. I'm meeting my—a friend there."

"You don't have much with you." She nodded at his backpack. "You ever been to a gathering?"

"No, it was kind of a spur of the moment thing. I'll be okay." He hoped he sounded more confident than he felt.

"I'm Ashley," she said, "but everybody calls me Ash."

"I'm—" He stopped, realizing he shouldn't give anyone his real name. He didn't want to put her or anyone else in a position where they'd have to lie if police came around asking about him. "I'm Hawk."

"Hawk?"

He remembered what River had said. "It's my rainbow name."

She let out a soft laugh. "Yeah, Glen had a rainbow name too."

"Is he your boyfriend?"

She shook her head. "It's not like that. We're best friends, been traveling together for about a year now. Our car broke down a few months ago, so we've been hitching rides."

The things she said made him feel guilty about the four brand new vehicles in his parents' four car garage, including his Mustang that he no longer had the keys to.

"Well, this is my ride right now," he said, nodding toward his bike.

"It's better than what I have," she sighed.

"Do you want to travel together, at least until we get to the gathering? It would be nice not to be alone."

"What about your bike?"

"I can hide it in the woods and come back for it after the gathering."

"It probably won't be here by then."

He shrugged. "I'll take my chances."

It was almost completely dark when they walked out to the road. A few vehicles passed them, but Talon guessed that not as many people came to the gathering at night. It would be harder to find your way around and to set up camp.

After two hours of walking, Talon was exhausted from everything that had happened that day. He was too tired to hide anymore every time a car drove by. Ash slowed down too, her shoulders drooping under the weight of her backpack. He'd offered to carry it a few times, but she refused.

"I don't think we'll make it there tonight," he said.

"Maybe not."

But Ash didn't stop. She put her head down, and if anything, picked up her pace. He admired her spirit.

A half hour later, he was about to ask her to stop when a van came up the hill and pulled alongside them. A middle-aged guy with a beard stuck his head out the window. There was a woman in the passenger seat and two more women in the second row seats. "You need a ride?"

Talon looked at Ash, unsure of what to do.

"Yeah, thanks," Ash said.

Talon followed Ash and climbed in through the side door. He climbed over some backpacks and gear, then flopped down on an empty seat in the very back. His back screamed at him, but he tried to shut out the pain. He listened while the guy—

who introduced himself as Jeff—talked to Ash, but Talon was too tired, too overwhelmed to talk. It wasn't long before he nodded off.

Talon woke when the van bounced over rough ground. He sat up and peered out the front window at what must have been the parking area. Cars and vans and busses were everywhere, endless lines of them. Jeff finally pulled into an open space.

Talon was the last one to get out. He heard voices and laughter and the faraway sound of music. Ash walked over to him. "You want to come with me? I'm gonna try to find some friends from last year who said they'd be up by Turtle Soup."

He had no idea what that meant. "No, but thanks. I need to try to find my friend."

"Do you know where to look?" she asked.

He nodded. Hopefully he'd find someone who knew where the dirty kids would be. As he looked around at all the cars and all the people, he wondered how he'd find anything or anyone.

Ash surprised him by giving him a hug. "I hope I see you around. Lovin you, brother." She thanked Jeff for the ride, then headed off on her own.

Talon walked up to Jeff, who was organizing backpacks and supplies he'd pulled from the van. "Uh, thanks for the ride."

"No problem. I'm glad I had room for you. My wife and I come every year—try to help as many of you kids as we can."

Talon's pulse quickened. If Jeff came to the gathering every year, he knew things. "You wouldn't happen to know where the dirty kids are, would you?"

"Not off hand, but somebody on the main trail should know." He turned and squinted like he was trying to see through the darkness. "If I've got my bearings right, Main Trail should be off that way. I think we're gonna stay here by the van tonight and hike in tomorrow when it's light. You're welcome to stay."

"No thanks, I need to find my friend."

Jeff looked at Talon's backpack. "Do you even have a flashlight in there? It's not easy to find your way in the dark."

Talon looked down and shook his head. He wished he had the camping gear that was back in his dad's car. He wished he had more water and something to eat.

Jeff went around to the front of the van and came back with a small flashlight. He handed it to Talon. "It's not great, but it's better than nothing."

"Thanks for everything," Talon said.

"If you change your mind and want to stay here for the night, you know where to find us."

Talon thanked him again and headed in the direction of the main trail.

It felt like he walked more than a mile past thousands of parked vehicles. He passed plenty of other people. Unlike him, none of them seemed lost. A lot of them met him with the words, "Welcome home." If the situation were different, if he wasn't exhausted and freezing, dehydrated and hungry, the sentiment might have made him feel good, but the farther he walked, the more lost and alone he felt. Every time he asked someone about the main trail, they told him to keep walking and he'd eventually get there. Some people he passed were drunk and harassed him. This wasn't how he imagined the gathering.

He wasn't sure how long he walked until he got to a place where a Handicamp sign was posted. It was the first place that looked like there was any type of camp. He walked up to an old guy standing by a beat-up camper. "Do you know where the dirty kids are?"

"You probably passed some of them in the parking area," the guy said.

"I'm looking for where they're camped."

"Not sure where that would be," the guy said. "The Welcome Home kitchen is about a mile up the main trail. They're one of the first kitchens you'll find. Just keep asking, someone will know."

Talon wanted to sit down and cry. He couldn't imagine walking another mile straight uphill at 10,000 feet. He was used to the altitude of Heber, but this was over four thousand feet higher.

"Thanks," Talon mumbled.

"Welcome home," the guy said as Talon trudged forward.

The hike to the Welcome Home kitchen was almost too much for him. Rocks littered the trail, and they were hard to see in the dark. The little flashlight helped, but it wasn't very powerful.

When he finally reached Welcome Home, he asked some people about the dirty kids. They pointed him further up the trail and told him to watch for a sign where the trail forked.

After more hiking and asking, he finally found some people who called themselves dirty kids. He squinted at a group that was gathered around a fire, and tried to pick out any familiar faces from the convenience store in Heber but he couldn't see them well enough. He walked up to a young woman who stood near the trail. "I'm looking for a friend of mine who said he'd been traveling with some of you," Talon said. "His name's River."

His heart galloped with anticipation. Running away, hiding, hiking, freezing—it would all be worth it when he saw River again.

"I don't know any River." She looked over her shoulder and yelled back to a group of people sitting around a fire. "Any of you know someone named River?"

No one did.

It didn't seem real. He couldn't have come all this way and gone through so much just to come up empty handed. He made his way to the group around the fire. "He came with some other people who were in busses. A rainbow colored bus and a dark blue one."

One of the guys laughed. "There's at least fifty busses that look like that back in Bus Village."

His heart plummeted to his feet. "Where's Bus Village?"

"You go back down Main Trail and head toward the parking area. Then you head east, no—" He shook his head.

"Or is it west? Who the fuck knows. You'll see them though, a shitload of busses."

Talon turned around, too discouraged, too fried to say thanks. He made it to the side of the trail and sank down on the ground. As dark and as late as it was, there were still people out on the trail. Almost all of them were walking with other people, talking, laughing, oblivious to him.

"Hey." It was the young woman with the dirty kids. She knelt in front of him and ran her hand through his hair. He was too tired to pull away. "You could stay here tonight," she said in an alluring voice, then moved closer to him.

It was enough to make him stand up. "I've gotta go," he mumbled.

He stumbled back to the main trail, then headed down the rocky path, making it past Welcome Home kitchen. Not long after that, his legs gave out. He half walked, half crawled to a little clearing a few yards off the trail where he collapsed. He'd never been so hungry, so thirsty, so tired. So hopeless.

Although it was pointless, Talon opened his backpack hoping there was something else in there to eat, a granola bar or something he'd forgotten about. There was nothing except a few books he hoped they'd let him keep at LIGHT along with some notebooks to write in. None of those things would ease his hunger or thirst or keep him warm.

The night was like torture. He lay on the ground, huddled in a ball, shivering. Even when he slipped into a semi-state of sleep, the cold followed him. In all of his dreams he was stuck in the snow or had fallen into icy water. There were several times throughout the dark night when he was sure the cold would kill him. All he had for warmth was River's sweatshirt. Although he could have gone out to the trail and asked for help, he didn't have the will or the energy. Nothing worked out like it was supposed to.

The whole time Talon had been in the dumpster, he'd played out the fantasy over and over. He'd get to the Rainbow Gathering and someone would show him right where the dirty kids camped. It wouldn't be miles up a steep, rocky trail. Once he got there, he'd ask about River. Before anyone could answer, River would hear him, and he'd run out to meet Talon. They'd hug, and River would kiss him like he did in the park.

He chided himself for being so stupid and romantic, for not thinking things through. He should have gone with Ash or stayed with Jeff for the night, but he was so sure he'd find River. Now he wondered if River was even there, or if River even really cared if he ever saw Talon again.

##

Thursday, July 2

By the time the first morning light pushed through the cold, dark sky, Talon felt like an idiot. As magic as that night in the park was with River, it was probably only magical for him. River wasn't stupid and naïve like Talon. It was clear that River had lived a lot more, had a lot more experience. River probably didn't even give Talon a second thought after he left the park.

The dawn should have brought some relief, but it did nothing for his hunger, his thirst, his spirit. And it was still fucking freezing. The trail was quiet now, except for a few people who wandered by. No one seemed to notice him off to the side, suffering. He had no idea he could feel this alone, this desolate with thousands of other people sharing the forest with him. But it didn't feel like they were sharing it. It seemed like they were all on the inside of something wonderful and secret, somewhere he didn't belong. No one else seemed lost like him.

He crawled over to an aspen tree and leaned against it, still shivering. The bark bit at the welts on his back, making everything worse. The knife in his backpack called to him. River had given him hope, kept him alive, but that was a fairytale he'd made up in his head. There was nothing for him at the Rainbow Gathering. And the only thing that waited for him back home was a prison where people would strip him, wipe him clean, make him into something unrecognizable. Either way, he was dead.

The knife handle was cold, but there was something soothing about holding it, something almost seductive. At least this would be his choice. He'd get to take his own life before someone at a dark place called LIGHT would take it from him.

The soft sound of a mandolin played from somewhere up the trail. Talon closed his eyes and listened for a moment, the music bringing a hint of sweetness to everything else that was bitter and cold. As the music drew nearer, Talon placed the knife against his wrist, looking at the path he'd make up his forearm. He closed his eyes for a few moments and noticed the music had stopped. He wished it hadn't. It would have been the one soothing thing as he left the world.

He opened his eyes and focused on his wrist as he pushed the knife in. It was like being outside of himself, like he was watching it happen to someone else. Somewhere in his head he thought it should hurt worse. Blood pooled around the blade and he went to pull it up his forearm.

"Hey, brother."

The soft voice made Talon stop and look up.

An older man walked off the trail toward him. He walked with a slow gait, one of his hands held out like he was approaching a scared animal. A mandolin was strapped around his shoulder and hung at his side.

A strange mixture of relief and anger flooded Talon as he looked at the man.

"Hey there, brother," the man said again.

Talon still held the knife but brought it down to his side. He looked from the blood dripping from his gash to the man coming toward him.

The man stopped and squatted down a few feet away from Talon. "You look like you could use a friendly face."

Talon let the knife fall and put his head in his hands. He was long past knowing what he needed. It felt like he should cry, like he should scream and tears should drown him, but nothing came out.

The sound of the guy coming closer made Talon look up again. "Let's have a look at that," the guy said, nodding at Talon's arm where blood still flowed from the wound. It made Talon wonder how deep he'd cut. It wasn't bleeding fast, but it was bleeding enough.

The old man held his hands out. They were as dirty as his clothes. He looked weathered and worn like life had taken a few bites out of him, gnawed at him around the edges. Seeing some of his own loneliness reflected in this man made Talon give in and hold his arm out.

The guy pulled a water bottle from his belt. "Need to clean it off, get a better look at it," he said in the same calm voice.

Talon nodded. He flinched a little when the icy water poured over the gash, which was about an inch long.

Without a word, the guy stripped off his dirty jacket, his sweater, and then the ragged T-shirt beneath it. He took the T-shirt and tore it into strips. "Need to get some pressure on it, wrap it up. You're not gonna bleed to death though."

Talon could only nod again while he watched the guy wrap several strips of the T-shirt around the wound, then he tied it off tight. Talon eyed the water bottle that sat on the ground a few inches away.

The guy noticed and handed the bottle to Talon. "Not too fast," he said when Talon began to gulp the water.

While Talon drank, the guy pulled his sweater and jacket back on and sat quietly until Talon finished drinking. As good as the water tasted, it wasn't enough. There wasn't enough water anywhere to quench his thirst.

Finally, he set the empty bottle down. "Thanks," he whispered to the man.

The guy nodded, then he held out his hand. "They call me Coyote Joe."

"I'm Talon." As soon as he said it, he realized he'd used his real name. At this point, he was too far gone to care. He took Coyote Joe's hand. In his calloused, weathered hand, there was something kindred like they might have shared the same pain. That connection grounded Talon, brought him back to himself. Coyote Joe's, dirty, lonely, gentle hand on his broke through and gave Talon the space, the safety to let his tears fall.

Coyote Joe didn't say anything when Talon finally wiped his eyes, just gave him a small nod, then stood up. "Let's get you some more water, something to eat. Then I know somebody who can look at your arm. She'll patch you up better than I did."

He held out his hand to Talon and helped him up. Talon leaned down and grabbed his backpack and knife.

Coyote Joe looked at the knife. "You want me to hold that for you?"

Talon shook his head and put the knife back in his pack. He looked at the old man, his eyes watering again. "Thanks," was all he managed to say.

"No need to thank me," Coyote Joe said, sounding uncomfortable. "My family's about two miles up the trail near Lovin' Ovens, but we'll stop on the way to get you something to eat, warm you up by a fire too."

Talon was surprised to hear Coyote Joe had a family. Everything about him screamed of being alone.

They hadn't been on the main trail for long when the smell hit Talon. Potatoes and meat and spices wafted through the air, making his mouth water. The smell was so intoxicating, he thought he was hallucinating.

He was surprised how close the Welcome Home kitchen was from where he'd ended up last night. A big sign that hung like a banner from the trees read WELCOME HOME in big colorful letters. He'd missed it last night in the dark. A group of people were gathered around a makeshift kitchen set up in the woods. A few people cut vegetables and put them in a metal barrel. Talon peeked in and saw what looked like the makings of some kind of stew. Other people were frying a big batch of chopped potatoes and onions with a little bit of meat mixed in.

An older guy with a long gray beard looked up from the potatoes and gave Coyote Joe a warm smile. "Coyote Joe, welcome home, brother." He walked over and gave Coyote Joe a hug. "When'd you get here?"

"A few days ago. I've been looking for you. Wasn't sure you'd make it this year."

The guy shook his head. "I'll be coming home until they put me in the ground." He gave Talon a questioning look, but Talon had no idea what to say. "You pick up a stray?" the guy asked Coyote Joe.

"Found him in the woods. He could use a little something to eat and some coffee to warm him up." Coyote Joe looked at Talon. "Talon, meet Ranger."

"Nice to meet you," Talon said in a soft voice. He still felt like an outsider.

Ranger reached for Talon's outstretched hand, but instead of shaking it, he pulled Talon into a bear hug. "Welcome home," Ranger said. He glanced at Talon's lightweight backpack. "This your first gathering?"

Talon nodded. He was glad his makeshift bandages were hidden beneath the sweatshirt. The last thing he wanted to do was answer questions about his arm.

"You're with good people," Ranger said. "If you've got a plate, we'll get you some breakfast."

"I don't... I didn't... I don't have one."

"Don't have one?" Ranger said like he'd committed a crime. Then he laughed a deep, rich laugh that filled the air and rustled the trees. He nodded at Talon's pack. "I doubt you have much of what you need in that thing."

"No, it was—I, um—I—" Talon's face burned.

"Give the kid a break," Coyote Joe said.

Ranger clapped Talon on the shoulder. "I'm just giving you some shit. You can use my plate."

Ranger pulled out a fork and a dented metal plate that looked as old as he was. He heaped it full of the potato casserole and handed it to Talon.

"Thanks." There should have been a bigger word, a better word than thanks.

He took the plate and sat in the sun on a fallen tree just a few feet away. Coyote Joe filled his water bottle at a water station, brought it to Talon, then walked back over to Ranger.

Although some of the vegetables were singed, and he had no idea what kind of meat was in the casserole, it was the best food Talon had ever eaten. By the time he finished the heaping portion, he was so full he felt sick.

He sat back for a moment and watched everyone at the kitchen talk while they fixed more food. It was still early, but a few people trailed in and got something to eat. Coyote Joe played a few songs on the mandolin. The sweet sound of the mandolin mixed with Coyote Joe's gravelly voice was strangely soothing.

As the food settled in Talon's stomach, a little of his energy returned and his head felt clearer. So much of last night was still a nightmarish fog.

When Talon walked back to the kitchen, Ranger showed him where the wash station was to clean the dishes. A few more people stopped by and jumped in to help make breakfast. Talon looked at Ranger. "Can I help with anything?"

Ranger nodded toward the big barrel of stew. "Help Rosemary with the welcome home stew. We went through a whole batch of it yesterday."

Talon was quiet while he chopped carrots and onions, content to listen to everyone around him talk.

He would have been happy to spend the morning at Welcome Home, working and listening to everyone, but it wasn't long before Coyote Joe came and got him. "We need to get that arm taken care of," he said so only Talon could hear.

They said goodbye to everyone at Welcome Home and headed up the trail.

The two-mile hike took a long time. Sometimes Coyote Joe needed to rest, sometimes it was Talon. A lot of people knew Coyote Joe and stopped to talk to him. Talon was content to quietly take it all in.

When one of the steep inclines gave way to some flatter ground, Talon heard a group of voices yell from somewhere in the distance, "We love you!" They drew out the word 'love' so it sounded like a song.

A moment later, the call was answered by other voices near and far with the same words, "We looooooove you!"

The call was echoed over and over until the trees and the mountains were alive with it.

Talon turned his face to the sun which had already warmed the air by at least ten degrees. It was the first time he'd really smiled since he'd gotten there. "It wasn't like this last night," he said, remembering how alone and cold and disconnected he'd felt.

Coyote Joe stopped and looked up the trail like he was studying something. "Yeah, it was."

Talon shook his head. "No, it wasn't."

Coyote Joe's eyes settled on Talon. "The gathering was the same. You were different. Two people can walk into the gathering side by side and walk away with completely different experiences. It's not the gathering, it's you."

Talon still wasn't so sure, but he didn't want to argue.

When it grew later in the morning, the trails began to fill up. He wondered how Coyote Joe knew where to go. There were trails that forked off, cardboard signs with arrows that read Bread of Life Kitchen, Kid Village, Main Meadow, CALM, Info. When he saw a sign for Turtle Soup, he thought about Ash and hoped she'd made it there last night.

When they reached the Info place near the Main Meadow, there was something that looked like a makeshift billboard with all kinds of dates and times and activities posted on it. No vehicles were allowed on the trail, so Talon had no idea how the kitchens and everyone else got all of their supplies and equipment up into the national forest.

"How much farther?" Talon asked after they'd walked for another twenty minutes.

"Not much. Just up beyond that next hill." He looked at Talon's arm with concern. "We probably shouldn't have stayed so long at Welcome Home."

Talon looked down at the blood that had soaked through his sweatshirt sleeve. Coyote Joe tore more strips from the torn T-shirt and wrapped them over the others that were now blood soaked.

The last part of the hike was the hardest. Fatigue set in again and Talon felt lightheaded. He was just about to ask to rest when Coyote Joe pointed and said, "It's just over there."

As they made their way to the kitchen, the smell of fresh baked bread hit him, making his mouth water. As full as he'd been earlier, he was starting to get hungry again. Instead of stopping at the kitchen, they took a smaller side trail and wound through a maze of tents, hammocks, and tarps. They neared a blond guy playing the guitar. A blonde woman slept in a sleeping bag on the ground next to him.

"Morning," the blond guy said to Coyote Joe. He gave Talon a curious look.

Coyote Joe looked at the woman. "She doing okay?"

The woman stirred and sat up. "*She's* doing fine, just resting in the sun."

Coyote Joe put his hand on Talon's shoulder. "I've got a brother who could use a little help. This is Talon."

The woman stood and gathered her messy hair in a ponytail. "I'm Maddy." She nodded to the guy with the guitar. "And this is Duncan, my…" She crinkled her forehead and looked at Duncan. "What are we?"

Duncan grinned. "I don't know, but at least we're a we."

Maddy rolled her eyes and turned her attention back to Talon. "Are you hurt or sick?" Maddy asked.

"Hurt," he mumbled. Why had Coyote Joe brought him so far up the trail to see some random woman?

"Come over here in the sun so I can have a look."

He hesitated, mainly because he didn't want to answer any questions she might ask about the gash on his forearm.

"Don't worry," Maddy said. "I'm a doctor. Well, I'm not practicing anywhere right now, but it hasn't been that long since I've been through med school and internships, so you're pretty safe with me."

The smile she gave him reassured him enough to walk over to her.

They sat on her sleeping bag while Coyote Joe sat on a stump near Duncan. Talon pulled up the sweatshirt sleeve to reveal the bandages. Blood had begun to seep through the newest ones.

"I patched him up a little," Coyote Joe said. "Cleaned it a little with water—didn't have anything else with me. Thought you might be able to help him."

Maddy pulled the bandages off one by one until she got to the wound. Talon steeled himself for the inevitable question, but it never came. Instead, Maddy turned to Duncan.

"Can you get the first aid kit from my backpack?"

Duncan nodded and disappeared into a tent.

When he came back with the first aid kit, Maddy worked at cleaning Talon's wound. It continued to bleed even after she put more pressure on it. It didn't bleed nearly as much as it had at first, but Maddy looked concerned. "When did this happen?" she asked.

He looked at the ground. "Early this morning, just after sunrise."

"It's pretty deep, and if it's been bleeding that long, you need stitches." She shook her head. "I don't have anything with me for stitches."

Talon's stomach lurched and he felt lightheaded. If he had to go to the hospital or a clinic in Heber, they'd have his information on file and would see that he was a minor and call his family. "I—I can't go to town to see a doctor, not yet, not now. Isn't there something else you can do?"

Maddy put a hand on his shoulder. "I don't have the stuff here, but the people at CALM should."

"I don't know what that is."

"It's where you go if you get sick or hurt while you're here. Coyote Joe could have taken you there too."

Coyote Joe gave Maddy some kind of look that Talon didn't understand. "I thought he might feel more comfortable up here. There were already a bunch of people waiting around CALM."

"It's okay," Maddy said. "I'm happy to help. I just wish I had what I needed. I can walk down to CALM and see if they'll let me have what I need." She looked at Talon. "You need to keep pressure on it the whole time I'm gone, okay?"

He nodded, but all he wanted to do was lay down and sleep now that he wasn't freezing and hungry. He wasn't sure if it was the blood loss or fatigue or both, but he began to feel removed again. Thinking beyond the moment was too overwhelming. Even though he seemed to have found some good people at the gathering, it didn't solve any of his problems. Once the gathering was over, he'd have no money, no place to stay. Nothing. He wasn't even sure if he had a place to stay at the gathering. Without a tent, or at least a sleeping bag, it wasn't realistic to stay there. Earlier, when he naively thought he'd be with River, he assumed River would at least have some kind of shelter and some blankets or sleeping bags.

In a lot of ways he was just as screwed now as he'd been when he'd cut himself this morning. The gravity of it swirled around him like a tornado, making him dizzy. Everything grew fuzzy and the ground tilted. Thankfully he was sitting, so he didn't have far to fall.

Voices surrounded him, encased him. Bits and pieces of what they said registered in his head. "Talon? You okay? Talon?" Then there was the voice that said, "…get him into town… lost too much blood… need to get help."

He opened his eyes and tried to sit up but couldn't. "No, I'm fine." He wished his voice sounded stronger.

"You're not fine," Duncan said, looking worried. He helped Talon sit up again.

"I can't go back to town. I can't."

Coyote Joe came into focus in his periphery vision. "Let's at least wait for Maddy to get back. The boy's not going to bleed to death."

"How do you know?" Duncan asked, sounding a lot less certain.

"Seen plenty of men bleed to death in Korea. He's lost blood, but not enough to die." Coyote Joe handed the water bottle to Talon. "You need to drink, stay hydrated."

Duncan sighed and sat back, still looking uncertain. He turned to Talon. "Did something happen back in town?" He looked at Talon's arm. "Did somebody there do—"

Coyote Joe thankfully interrupted. "He'll tell us when he wants to. If he wants to."

It wasn't much longer before Maddy came back. By the time she stitched up his arm, he was exhausted. Maddy must have noticed. "You need to rest. Did you bring a tent?"

Talon shook his head. "I don't have much. I had to leave in kind of a hurry."

He worried she'd ask him why, but she didn't. He was thankful that she and Coyote Joe seemed to sense that he didn't want to talk about it.

"I know someone who has some extra gear," Coyote Joe said to him. "I got a ride here with them. They're good people."

"Nate and Kita?" Maddy asked.

Coyote Joe nodded.

"I saw them working in the kitchen on my way back up here."

Talon barely remembered meeting Nate and Kita, barely remembered Kita saying she had a tent and sleeping bag she wasn't using. All he remembered was crawling into the tent and collapsing on the sleeping bag.

Someone called to him in his dream. The way she said his name was sweet, so it wasn't his mom. "Talon."

Someone shook his shoulder. "Talon."

When he opened his eyes, Maddy's face and long blonde hair came into focus. His mouth was dry and he felt like he'd been run over by a tank. His arm ached, but his back hurt worse where his dad had beaten him.

The look of shock on Maddy's face caught him off guard. "Jesus, Talon, what happened to you? Who did this to you?!"

Then he remembered taking his shirt off sometime during the afternoon when the sun beat down on him through the tent. His stomach somersaulted and he frantically looked for his shirt, needing to cover up the marks that seeped with too many questions.

"It's nothing," he muttered, wincing as he pulled his T-shirt on.

Maddy sat back and closed her eyes for a few moments like she was about to meditate. Then she looked at him with compassion, like she was somehow a sister in his pain. "I get it," she said. "I get not wanting to talk about it, and I'm trying not to ask too many questions, but that…" She motioned to his back. "That's messed up. Whoever did that to you shouldn't get away with it."

As nice and as understanding as she seemed, he wasn't about to tell her anything about his arm or his back. "I'm fine. I'll be fine."

Maddy sighed and nodded. "If you ever want to talk, I'll listen. So will Duncan or Coyote Joe.

"Thanks, but I'm—"

"Fine," she finished. "I know all about being 'fine.'"

He wanted to ask her what she meant, but he bit back the question.

"How are you feeling? How's your pain?" she asked. "And don't give me some bullshit answer about feeling fine because you look like hell."

He couldn't help but smile. There was something about her directness, her honesty that he liked. "I feel like shit. Like I just walked through hell," he whispered.

"I've got some ibuprofen if you want some."

"Yeah."

"They're gonna serve supper in the main meadow. We thought you'd like to go. We can always bring something back for you, but the first night I had supper with everyone in the meadow…" She got a faraway look in her eyes. "Well, you have to experience it for yourself."

He was glad she'd quit asking personal questions. "I'll go with you."

He made his way to the main meadow with Coyote Joe, Maddy and Duncan, Kita and Nate, and another couple named Campbell and Rain. A few other people he hadn't officially met walked with the group.

"We all got to the gathering a day or two early and ended up meeting when we all camped near Lovin' Ovens," Maddy told him as they made their way to the meadow.

There were even more people at the gathering now. As they hiked down the hill, a sea of people made their way to the main meadow. There was such a diverse mix of people he'd never seen together anywhere else. People of every age, from babies to people who looked older than Coyote Joe or Ranger. People dressed in old, worn clothes stood beside people in expensive hiking gear who stood beside people decked out in colorful costumes. Other people didn't bother to wear clothes.

There was so much to take in from the people to the music. But the one thing he wanted most was missing. He scanned the crowd but didn't see River. To have River beside him in that moment would have been perfect. Nate and Kita had introduced Talon to a young couple—Sonny and Ripple—who reminded him of the people River had been with. Talon was tempted to ask them if they knew the dirty kids and River, but he wasn't ready for more disappointment.

Maddy was right about the experience in the main meadow. Several people spoke before they ate, then everyone stood and held hands. The sound of "ohm" rose from the group—some voices low and rich, some high and sweet. The voices all united in harmony to create a beautiful ohm that connected all of them. The ohm rose above the meadow, enveloping them until it was carried away on the wind and consumed by the mountains. It was the closest Talon came to peace and happiness since he'd been with River.

All of the people from various kitchens had carted food to the meadow and brought it around, serving it to everyone. Coyote Joe had an extra plate and silverware that he loaned to Talon.

After he ate, Talon found a big rock to sit on off to the side of the meadow. Coyote Joe played his mandolin. Maddy and Duncan joined him with their guitars, along with an old guy playing the banjo. Kita and Nate sat a few yards away talking to Rain and Campbell. As nice as they'd all been to him, he still felt alone.

He closed his eyes and tried to enjoy the music, tried not to think about what would happen after the gathering.

"Talon?"

He opened his eyes to see Kita sitting down next him.

"I just wanted to let you know that you can use my tent and sleeping bag for as long as you need to. I, um, I've been staying with Nate, so I don't need it right now."

"Thanks. I didn't—well I—I wasn't—" He shook his head. "I didn't plan very well. I guess I didn't plan at all. I mean I wanted to come to the gathering, but things got kind of crazy and I didn't get a chance to pack anything."

Kita gave him a kindred smile. "You and me both, except I had no idea what a Rainbow Gathering even was." She looked around the meadow, then her eyes stopped at Nate. "I never planned to be here, never dreamed I'd do something this impulsive and crazy."

He couldn't help but smile back at her. "I'm glad to know I'm not the only one. Can I ask how you ended up here?"

Kita didn't go into a lot of detail, but she told him that her marriage was over and that she and her daughter needed a break from each other. She told him about her chance meeting with Nate, Sonny, and Ripple who were on their way to the gathering, and her spur of the moment decision to go with them.

"You mean you and Nate haven't known each other very long?"

She shook her head. "Not even quite a week yet. It feels like longer though."

Hearing her talk about Nate, seeing the connection between them made Talon feel less crazy about his feelings toward River. He just wished those feelings had been reciprocated like they were with Nate and Kita.

"I hope after some time apart, my daughter will be ready to talk, to try to work through some things." Kita traced the cracks in the rock with her finger. "She's around your age."

He wondered what had come between Kita and her daughter—she didn't seem closed minded or judgmental like his parents, but maybe she just hid it better. "Did she do something that made you mad? That made you leave?"

Kita turned her face to the sky like she was looking for answers. "You know, I've thought a lot about it these past few days, and it's more about me than it is about Georgia. I can't figure out if I did too much for her or not enough. I hope I can figure that out while I'm here." She turned to face him. "I don't know what happened, why you had to leave in such a hurry, but if you ever want to talk about it, I'll listen. Anyone in our group will."

"Thanks." A part of him wanted to spill his guts to Kita, but he worried if any of them knew the full story and knew he wasn't eighteen yet, they'd try to make him go home. Except one person. "What do you know about Coyote Joe?"

"Not a lot. Nate picked him up in Utah on our way here. He's pretty quiet, but I trust him. I get the feeling he'd give you his shirt even if it was the last one he had."

"I think so too."

Kita placed a gentle hand on his shoulder. "I'm glad he brought you to us."

Talon gave a small nod. "Me too." He wondered if any of them knew that Coyote Joe had saved his life.

##

Saturday, July 4
Talon woke to the absence of voices. The only sounds he heard were the birds and people's footsteps as they walked by. Everyone had told him about the silence on July 4th that lasted from sunrise until noon, about gathering in the main meadow where everyone would join hands in a silent prayer or meditation for peace.

After eating some fresh baked biscuits made from the earthen ovens at Lovin' Ovens, they all made their way to the main meadow. There were already thousands of people there forming a gigantic circle that stretched beyond the meadow, beyond Talon's line of sight.

He stood between Kita and Maddy, holding their hands. Unsure of what to do, he looked at the human chain that continued to grow as more and more people made their way to the meadow. Although this was a time for prayer, Talon didn't want to pray. His church had told his parents about LIGHT. The older he got, the more hypocritical his church seemed. They preached love in one breath, then exclusion and hell in the next.

Since he didn't know anything about meditating, and he wasn't going to pray, Talon studied everyone he could see in the circle. Some people stood with their eyes closed. Others looked lost in thought. Some smiled. Some people danced or blew bubbles. Everyone seemed to have their own way of being, which made him feel more comfortable with just standing there, watching.

The longer he watched, the more connected, the more accepted he felt. He'd never seen a more diverse group of people—people from all classes, all races, probably all religions—holding hands in love, in peace. He'd seen plenty of gay couples over the past two days. This was a place where they could just be and not have to worry about judgment or hatred. It would be nice if the real world was like a Rainbow Gathering.

Any sense of time got lost as he melded into the circle, joining with everyone there, even the people he couldn't see.

And he loved them all, loved their flaws and their beauty. For the first time in years, he felt truly loved, just for being him. It didn't matter that he'd lived a lie, that he was gay, that his family was ashamed of him. These people loved him. Maddy and Kita's hands pulsed with that love—the love that was carried from hand to hand to hand and back to him. He just hoped they all felt his love too.

Then someone started an ohm and all of the voices joined in until there was an endless chain, an endless circle of ohm rising from the meadow. Talon's voice melded with all the others, becoming one beautiful voice from one beautiful source.

The faint sound of children singing made him think he was hallucinating. Then he turned to see all the children run down the hill toward the circle, their beautiful voices breaking the silence as they broke through the circle.

Laughter and talking and singing filled the once silent meadow. Talon smiled at the children whose faces were painted. It tugged at his heart because his sister, Delphine, would have loved this. His eyes burned with the pain of missing her. Despite what his parents had done, there were things he missed about them. He missed how they were with him before they found out.

Maddy's arms were around him, pulling him back to the moment. "Lovin' you, brother," she said, holding him tight.

"You too," he whispered, trying to find his voice.

Then Duncan hugged him and Kita and Nate and everyone else he'd met and so many people he hadn't met. And he was loved.

A few moments later, Rain pulled him aside. Her auburn hair was pulled back in a loose braid, and the expression on her face was a strange mixture of peace and sorrow. "I've been thinking about you," she said.

His stomach dropped. It sounded like she was about to pry into things he wasn't ready to talk about. "Oh?"

"You can tell me it's none of my business if you want to," she said, tucking some flyaway hair behind her ear. "I keep wondering if you have a place to stay after the gathering is over."

Talon shrugged. He didn't, and he had no idea what to do about it. He'd overheard Sonny and Ripple talk about the road, about where they'd go next. He thought about asking if he could tag along, but he wasn't sure if that was the kind of life he wanted. He'd also wondered about Coyote Joe and where he was headed next, if he had a place to call home.

"Well," Rain said, "if you don't have anywhere to go, will you tell me? I've been thinking a lot about it and I might be able to help—I mean Campbell and I might be able to help."

Talon looked at the ground. "Thanks," he mumbled.

"We all care about you."

He nodded, but couldn't meet her eyes. He had no idea why a group of strangers would care anything about him.

"Do you want to walk back with us?" she asked, nodding toward Campbell who was waiting a few yards away.

"I think I'll stay here for a while," he said. He wanted to sit and absorb any energy that was left over from the circle.

##

Talon stayed in the meadow for a long time, long after everyone else in his group left. He found a rock to sit on off to the side of the meadow and closed his eyes. The ache of losing River clawed at his heart. River had been his hope, the person who gave him the courage to run from his parents, to go to the gathering. Now he was gone. Not just gone, he'd probably found someone else to hook up with.

Keeping his eyes closed he imagined River sitting beside him, holding his hand, their fingers entwined. He ached to feel that one more time. To feel River's mouth on his, his hand on Talon's thigh.

"Hawk?"

The name didn't register.

"Hawk?"

He opened his eyes to see Ash in front of him. He stood up and hugged her, feeling that connection to her too—his sister who traveled through the darkness with him. "Did you find your friends at Turtle Soup?" he asked.

They both sat on the rock. "Yeah, did you find your friend?"

He shook his head. "I guess he wasn't really my friend."

"I'm sorry, Hawk."

He looked at the ground. Now that everyone else he'd met knew his name, he might as well tell Ash. "My name's not Hawk. I don't really have a rainbow name, it was just something I made up. I'm Talon."

Her eyes widened. "You're him?"

"Who?" He had no idea what she was talking about.

"Glen wouldn't shut up about you."

"Who's Glen?"

She wrinkled her forehead. "Why didn't you tell me you were Talon?"

Nothing made sense. "Who's Glen?"

"Oh god," she said. "River. He told you his name was River, didn't he."

Talon stood up. Adrenaline poured through him, making his heart pound so loud, it echoed in his head. "He's your best friend? The one you were traveling with?" The adrenaline morphed into dread, making him lose his footing. "The one who got beat up? But you weren't at the gas station that night when I first met him."

Ash shook her head. "That guy who worked there was yelling at us and I didn't want any trouble, so I walked down the street and waited there. But that's not important." She hung her head. "River should have shown up here by now. I told him where I'd be and he promised to find me, but—"

"We have to find him," Talon interrupted.

Ash looked just as worried as he felt. "I know. I was gonna see if I could hitch a ride back to town to look for him."

Talon grabbed her hand and pulled her up. "I know someone I can ask. C'mon."

##

194

Maddy lay under a tree near her tent, her head resting on Duncan's leg.

"I need a favor," Talon blurted when he reached them. "I need a ride to town." He glanced at Ash. "We need a ride. This is my friend, Ash."

Ash said a shy hello.

As soon as Maddy sat up, Talon felt bad. She looked tired and a little pale. "Is everything okay?" she asked.

"I don't know," Talon said. His heart hadn't stopped its frantic beat since he'd talked to Ash in the meadow. "A friend of ours, he's in trouble and I think he needs our help. He's hurt and…please, we just need to find him and make sure he's okay."

Frown lines formed on Maddy's forehead. "Did this friend have anything to do with—you know—what happened to you?"

"No," he snapped. "He'd never—he's not like that." His dad's fury made the welts on Talon's back burn. His parents and his church and LIGHT put the knife in his hand, making him want to give up. River made him want to live, made him feel like there was some light in the world. But what if kissing River in the park had gotten him beaten up? He looked at Ash. "Am I the reason he's hurt?"

Ash sucked in an audible breath. "No you're not. Those assholes are the only ones to blame."

Talon ground the dirt with his heel. "But if I hadn't—if we hadn't, then maybe—"

"Bullshit," Ash hissed. Any sense of shyness disintegrated in the face of her fury. "Kissing someone shouldn't put you in the hospital. It's the twenty-first century for fuck's sake!"

Talon's face burned in the silence that surrounded them. Ash's outburst had gotten the attention of everyone around them. Attention Talon didn't want. He'd never said the words out loud, had never told anyone he was gay. Ever since he could remember, his family, his church had talked about that sin, burning the shame of it into his skin. He hated himself for still feeling that shame.

"Come on," Maddy said. "I'll take you to find your friend."

"You sure?" Duncan asked. "You need some rest."

Maddy gave him a sideways glance. "I can rest when I'm dead."

Duncan looked like she'd punched him, making Talon wonder what had just happened.

"Are you okay?" Talon asked Maddy. "If you don't feel well—"

"I'm fine," she barked.

Her answer made him think back to the day he'd gotten to the gathering and their conversation about being fine. Apparently he wasn't the only one hiding something.

Duncan stood too, his jaw set tight. "I know you're *fine*, but I'm going with you. I can drive. You just need to tell me where we're going."

"The hospital," Talon and Ash said at the same time.

##

It felt like it took hours to get to the hospital in Heber. The walk to the parking area was every bit as long as Talon remembered. Finding Duncan's car took almost as long.

When they finally parked in the crowded hospital parking lot, Talon's stomach lurched into his throat. The thought of seeing River again battled with the fear of getting caught. Almost everyone in Heber knew Talon's family. Someone at the hospital was bound to recognize him.

Despite the warmth of the day, he took River's sweatshirt and put it on, pulling the hood up, hoping it would help to hide his face. He turned to Ash. "Will you do the talking? I kinda need to keep a low profile."

Maddy turned around in the passenger seat and looked at him. "I hope you know by now that you can trust us."

He trusted them more than anyone else. He just didn't know what they'd do if they found out he wasn't eighteen yet. His eyes dropped to the floor. "The person who did—you know— Well, they might be here, and I don't want them to see me."

Duncan turned around, his eyes narrowed. "Did somebody hurt you?" He turned to Maddy. "Did somebody hurt him?"

"I don't want to talk about it," Talon mumbled. "I just want to find my friend."

"Okay, let's go," Maddy said.

"I think just Ash and I should go," Talon said. The fewer people who went inside with him, the less attention they'd draw.

"I might be able to help," Maddy said, "especially with any medical questions." Her voice was firm, making him look at her. "I'm on your side. Whatever's going on, I'm on your side."

"Okay," Talon sighed, "Come on."

When they walked in the front door, Talon pulled at the sweatshirt hood again and kept his eyes on the floor, hoping to hide his face.

"Do you know where his room is?" he whispered to Ash.

"No. He was still in the emergency room when I left."

"We can ask someone at the front desk," Maddy said, "but you'll have to tell them you're family. They probably won't tell you anything if you're not."

"Yeah, I told them I was his sister when they brought him here," Ash said.

Talon tried to swallow the lump of panic in his throat as they neared the information desk. Cindy Murphy—the old lady who played the organ at church—sat behind the desk.

"I'm gonna hang back here while you ask," Talon said to Ash.

"I'll go with Ash," Maddy said.

While Ash and Maddy waited in line, Talon sat in a chair off to the side and put his head down.

Once the gathering was over he needed to get out of Heber for good. He had no idea how he'd pull it off with no money and no place to go, but he couldn't go back home, even after he turned eighteen. Not after what his parents were going to do to him. Not after what his dad had done to him.

"Talon?"

Ash's voice made him jump. "What'd you find out?" he asked.

Ash looked just as worried now as she had at the gathering. "They said he's getting released, that we might have already missed him. We need to hurry, see if we can find him."

When they reached the floor where River was, they were told he'd left not long ago. Talon's eyes stung. The hope of getting to see River again felt like dust in his hands.

Maddy put a gentle hand on his shoulder. "We'll find him."

Ash nodded. "He'll be headed to the gathering. I know he will."

Their optimism should have bolstered him, but his body and spirit sagged under another defeat.

The weight of that defeat stayed with him as they made their way to the main entrance, Talon walking behind Maddy and Ash. As they walked past the administrative offices on the first floor, he heard a familiar deep laugh. His breath caught when he glanced through the glass walls of the office. He should have run, but he froze, staring at his dad who was looking over some papers with the CEO, who went to their church. For the past few months, his dad had been talking about closing a deal with the hospital, selling a piece of land to the them for a new freestanding clinic. It looked like he'd made the deal.

"Shit," Talon muttered under his breath, telling himself to run.

Maddy must have heard, and stopped to look back, giving him a questioning look.

In the second before Talon bolted, his dad looked up, looking as shocked, as surprised as Talon felt.

He wasn't frozen anymore. "Shit, shit, shit," he hissed, catching up to Maddy and Ash. "We need to go. Now!"

"Talon!" his dad's voice chased him down the hallway.

He stole a glance back to see his dad sprint out of the office after them. "Talon, wait!"

"Go, go, go!" Talon yelled. At least no one asked why. They must have sensed his fear because they were right on his heels.

It was impossible to run full speed through the crowded halls. Every time he had to slow down or swerve, he swore he felt his dad's fingers on his shoulders. He didn't dare look back, but footsteps pounded behind him. Every few seconds, his dad yelled his name.

When they ran out the front doors and into the parking lot, Talon sprinted toward Duncan's car. From close behind him, Maddy yelled, "Duncan, start the car! Start the car!"

Talon yelled too, praying Duncan could hear them.

Duncan's little Toyota rumbled to life just as Talon reached it. He flew into the back seat and looked up in horror to see his dad just a few yards behind Ash and Maddy.

"Go—as soon as they get into the car—go," Talon choked, his chest heaving.

A few seconds later, Ash launched herself into the back seat while Maddy got in the front.

Instead of stopping, Talon's dad veered and ran down another row of parked cars.

"Shit, he's going to follow us!" Talon yelled after he spotted his dad's black SUV in the lot.

"Will someone tell me what in the hell's going on?" Duncan ordered as he pulled out of the parking lot, his tires squealing.

"I don't know." Maddy's voice was full of concern. "Just get away from here."

"Where am I supposed to go?" Duncan asked as he drove away from the hospital.

Talon scrambled to think of a place that his dad didn't know about. "Turn left up there, just past the stoplight," he said, his heart still thundering. "Then go about five miles and you'll see a lane with a "for sale" sign by it. The gate's not locked. The place is old and abandoned." High school kids sometimes went there to party. It was far enough from town that they never got caught.

"What happened back there?" Duncan demanded. "Who was chasing you?"

Talon stole a look behind them to make sure they'd lost his dad. There was no sign of his car.

"Talon?" Duncan asked when Talon didn't answer.

"Just give him a minute," Maddy said.

Duncan gave him until they were through the gate of the deserted property and hidden at the far end of the lane. It didn't look like anyone ever came to take care of the land or the house. The two and a half story white house looked like it had been a decent place at one time, but now it was crumbling under the elements. Plants and weeds had grown wild, taking over the big yard. Behind the house was the old weathered barn where everyone partied.

Both Maddy and Duncan turned to look at Talon after they'd parked.

"Was that your dad?" Maddy asked.

Talon nodded and looked down at his hands. A piece of the bandage around his wrist peeked out from the sweatshirt sleeve.

"And he's the one who…?"

"He hurt you?" Duncan asked, sounding sick.

"Not my arm," Talon said. "But, well, Maddy knows what he did."

Ash gave Talon's hand a squeeze that made him feel like she knew exactly what he was going through.

"So they'll be looking for us now, looking for my car," Duncan said.

"Yeah." Talon felt bad about dragging them into his mess of a life. "I'm sorry. My dad's a bigwig. Everybody knows him. He's pretty tight with the cops."

"I'm gonna get charged with kidnapping, aren't I," Duncan said. At least he didn't sound mad about it, just kind of resigned.

"I'll be eighteen next month." As soon as he said it he realized it probably wouldn't make any difference to the police.

"I'll be eighteen next year," Ash said in a soft voice. "But nobody's looking for me."

The hurt and the truth in her voice made Talon's eyes burn. "You guys should go," Talon said to Maddy and Duncan. He squeezed Ash's hand like she'd just done with him. "Ash and I can manage. We'll find a way back to the gathering." And hopefully find River on their way while trying to stay out of sight. It would be dark pretty soon, which would make it easier to stay hidden.

"We're not leaving you." Maddy's voice was fierce. "We just need to figure out what to do."

"We should wait until it's dark," Duncan said.

Talon nodded, knowing he was right, but he hated the idea of River being out there alone.

"What about Glen?" Ash asked, giving Talon a worried look. "We need to find him."

"We will." Talon tried to sound more confident than he was.

"Is he from here too?" Duncan asked. "Your friend who was in the hospital?"

"No," Talon said. "I don't know where he's from. I, um, I just met him the other night." It was strange to say it out loud, strange to feel his heart surge and break and swell at the thought of someone he'd just met. "Ash has known him a lot longer."

"I don't know what I would have done without him," Ash said. "He's more of a brother, more like family than the family I had. And some assholes beat him up just cuz he's gay." She hung her head like she'd just given herself a life sentence for a crime. "I should've stayed with him in the hospital."

Maddy studied Talon like she was weaving pieces of a puzzle together. "Is that why you ran away?" she asked in a gentle voice. "Did your dad do that to you because he found out?"

He let out a sigh and nodded. In a way, it was a relief that she knew. "They were going to send me to one of those places where they try to pray it out of you or beat it out of you. Probably both. I read about them—how they try to brainwash you, use anything they can to make you straight."

"They're not gonna do that because we're gonna make sure they never find you," Duncan said, the sharp edge to his voice slicing through the air. "I thought we were past all this dark ages bullshit."

Talon was overwhelmed with gratitude. Everyone he'd met at the gathering had done so much for him. They'd given him shelter and food and friendship.

Family.

##

When darkness engulfed the abandoned acreage, they made their way back toward town.

"Any idea where we might find him?" Maddy asked.

"He's probably trying to catch a ride to the gathering," Ash said, "so we should just drive there and look for him."

"It won't be easy to see in the dark," Duncan said.

An idea tugged at Talon, even though it didn't make much sense. But it wouldn't let go of him. "Can we drive by the park?" Getting to the park put them right inside the town where there'd be a lot of people who might recognize him.

"Why?" Maddy asked.

"Because he might be there," Ash answered. She gave Talon a hint of a smile. "It's worth a shot."

"We can come at the park from the back," Talon said. "There's an alley a block or two away where you can park and wait. I should be able to sneak in and take a look around."

Talon directed Duncan through town avoiding the main roads, which would hopefully help them avoid the police. Twenty minutes later, they parked in the alley and Talon headed toward the park. There were more people there than he expected. A lot of them looked like people from the gathering, which probably meant police would be patrolling the area.

Talon put his head down and quickly walked toward the picnic table where he'd sat with River. From a distance, the tables looked empty, but it was hard to tell in that dark corner of the park. He told himself not to get his hopes up, that River could be anywhere. How in the hell was he supposed to find one person who could be anywhere between here and the gathering? One person among thousands and thousands.

When he got closer to the tables he stopped and squinted to make sure he wasn't seeing things. Someone lay on their back on top of the picnic table where he and River had sat just a few nights ago.

It might not be him. He took a step closer. *It's probably not him.* His heart thundered. *It can't be him.* But what if? "River," he said in a loud whisper.

The person on the table didn't move.

"River?" A little louder.

Still nothing.

Talon walked closer and noticed a backpack beneath the picnic table. It felt strange, intrusive to walk up to someone who was passed out or asleep, but he needed to know.

His thundering heart skidded to a halt when he saw a cast on the person's left forearm.

Nothing could keep him away. He closed the distance between him and the picnic table in just a few long strides. It was River's slender frame, his messy brown hair.

"River," he said loud enough to wake him.

River stirred, then winced as he startled awake and sat up. For a moment, he just stared at Talon, an awful moment when Talon was sure River didn't remember him, that their short time together had meant nothing. Although it was the moment when Talon woke up, it might have been just a blink in River's life. Then a look of disbelief morphed into a grin.

"I'm dreaming, aren't I," River said.

"It feels like it, doesn't it. I could pinch you if you want me to."

River's grin grew wider "There's a lot of other things I'd rather have you do to me."

Talon stepped closer, close enough to feel River's breath on his face. "You're really here."

River leaned forward, his forehead touching Talon's. "How'd you know?"

"I didn't know. I hoped."

River's lips were right there. "I wanted to be close to you, so I came here."

Talon kissed him then. The world shrank and it was just him and River clamoring to get closer, clamoring to close any space between them. River tasted like life, like earth, like love, like every fantasy Talon had ever had.

"That was even better than I remembered," Talon said when they finally stopped kissing.

"I didn't know if you'd—" River looked down. "If it meant—if you even cared if you saw me again."

"Are you crazy? I haven't stopped looking for you since that night."

River gave him a tired smile. "You got away—they didn't take you to that place."

Flashing red and blue lights down the street caught Talon's eye. "Yeah, just barely, but they're still looking for me. My dad saw me when I was looking for you at the hospital. I barely got away." The police car drew nearer. "We have to go. Now."

River sighed, looking nervous, but exhausted. "Where? I can't go far, man. I'm so fucking exhausted. They said my cut got infected—it's why they kept me in the hospital so long."

"What do you mean? I thought you broke your arm."

"Yeah, got stabbed too."

Talon's stomach lurched, making him nauseous.

Two police cars pulled up and parked by the front of the park where a group of people were partying.

"Can you make it a few blocks?" Talon asked, trying to stay calm as he watched the officers get out of their cars. "There are some people who can help you. And Ash…Ash is there too."

River sat up straighter. "Ash? How do you know her?"

Talon pulled his hood up and turned away from the officers who were already in a heated conversation with the partiers. One of the officers broke away and began to make her way through the park. "Long story," Talon whispered, "but we need to get out of here. We have company."

"Yeah, I see them. Shit."

Talon reached under the picnic table, grabbed River's pack, and hoisted it over his shoulders. The pain in his back was a little better, but he cringed when the weight of the backpack hit it.

River gingerly got down from the table, then grabbed it to steady himself. "Fuck," he muttered, "just give me a minute."

Talon nodded, although he wasn't sure they had a minute. The officer was getting closer. He grabbed River's arm and guided him forward. "C'mon, it's not far."

They'd only taken a few steps when he heard the policewoman from behind them. "Everything okay over here?" she asked.

Talon half turned, but kept his head down. "We're good, thanks."

"Is your friend drunk? High on something?" She was just a few yards away.

"Sick," Talon said, trying to keep his voice calm. "He just needs some rest."

"You need any help?"

He wanted to tell her to shut up and leave them alone. Instead, he took a breath. "No, we have friends we can crash with."

"Okay." The officer hesitated for a moment, then turned around.

"Fuck, that was too close," River said.

"Yeah, we need to get out of here."

River was out of breath by the time they reached Duncan's car. He stopped as soon as he saw Duncan and Maddy in the front. "Who are they?" he asked, sounding worried.

"You can trust them," Talon said. "They helped me when—" He remembered the way Maddy stitched his arm and didn't ask questions, remembered the way she and Duncan were still on his side even after they found out he was a runaway. "You can trust them. And Ash is in the back seat."

Except she wasn't in the back seat anymore. She flew out of the car and wrapped her arms around River. "You idiot," she said, her voice shaking, "I've been looking everywhere for you. You scared the shit out of me."

Maddy rolled down her window. "We really need to go," she said.

The three of them climbed into the back seat with River in the middle. Talon guided Duncan through the side streets and finally to the forest service road that led back to the gathering.

It was late at night by the time they parked. River was in and out of sleep, which worried Talon. River had seemed okay when he'd first gotten in the car, excited to be reunited with Ash and back with Talon, but that energy was short lived.

"I think we should crash in the car tonight," Talon said when he had trouble waking River. Ash seemed worried too. "I don't think he's feeling too great. He said something about getting an infection when he was in the hospital."

"Did they give him antibiotics?" Maddy asked. "They better have sent some with him."

"I don't know."

Talon gave River's shoulder a gentle shake. He moved, but didn't wake up. It took both Ash and Talon to finally rouse him.

"Sorry," Talon said, feeling bad for waking him. "Maddy wants to know if the doctor at the hospital sent any medicine with you."

River blinked a few times, looking confused as to where he was. When he saw Talon, the confusion melted away. "Yeah," he said in a scratchy voice. "But I don't know what it is." He reached into his coat pocket, pulled out a pill bottle, and handed it to Maddy.

She'd just taken the bottle when it fell out of her hand and onto her seat. "Dammit," she hissed, rubbing her hand.

Duncan turned to her looking worried. "Hey, are you okay? Do you need—"

"I'm fine, she snapped.

But Talon caught the expression on her face, and it was clear that Duncan was worried. It made him wonder again if Maddy was hiding something of her own, if there was something wrong with her. He wasn't sure he could handle it if someone else he cared about was hurt or sick.

"Do you want to stay here for the night?" Talon asked River. "That way you can rest and we can hike up in the morning."

River shook his head. "I don't want them to find you."

"It'll be okay," Talon said.

"You don't know that!" River snapped. "Sorry, I just…they can't find you. I'll be fine. I promise."

Maddy turned toward them. "We can just take it slow and easy and stop whenever somebody needs to rest."

It took a few hours to finally reach Lovin' Ovens. River had to stop and rest several times, which didn't surprise Talon. Sometimes it was Maddy who needed a break, which worried him. She was young and seemed healthy enough, but there were times that things didn't seem quite right.

Everyone went straight to their tents when they reached Lovin' Ovens. River fell asleep almost as soon as he was inside the sleeping bag. Talon sat a few feet away, trying to stay awake to keep an eye on him. Although Maddy had said he was probably okay, Talon worried.

As hard as he tried to stay awake, it wasn't long before he dozed in and out of sleep. He jolted awake when someone touched his arm. He panicked, thinking his dad had found him and was going to drag him away from the tent, away from River.

"Hey, man, it's just me," River said in a scratchy voice. "You been sitting there all night?"

A hint of light threaded the darkness. The drums pulsed through the woods. A few people talked in the distance. It was the sound of early morning, pre-dawn.

Talon stretched. "Yeah. I didn't mean to fall asleep though. I just—I wanted to make sure you were okay."

"I'm good."

"You sure? I can find Maddy, have her take a look at you just in case—"

"I'm fine," River interrupted. He unzipped the sleeping bag and slowly made his way to his feet.

"Where are you going?" Talon asked.

"I've gotta take a piss."

"Be careful," Talon said with a smirk. "I thought I was going to piss icicles when I went out a little bit ago."

"Great," River grumbled.

A few minutes later, River came back in, grabbed his sleeping bag, and sat beside Talon. "It's fuckin' freezin' up here," he said through chattering teeth.

"I warned you."

They opened the sleeping bag and put it over their shoulders, wrapping themselves in it. Talon leaned into River, wishing he knew what to do, how close he was supposed to get.

River let out a breath and leaned into him too. "I still can't believe you came looking for me."

Talon grinned. "Yeah, I kinda risked my life for you."

River looked down and shook his head. "You shouldn't have." His voice got softer. "It wasn't worth it."

Talon turned to River. "What do you mean? You're the one who gave me the guts to run away, to come here. If it weren't for you I'd be in some hellhole trying to figure out how to off myself. So don't ever say you weren't worth it."

River looked away for a few moments, making Talon wonder if he'd said something wrong, if he'd ruined whatever was between them. But when River looked at him again, his eyes looked like fire. "Come here," River said.

Talon got on his knees and closed the small distance between them. They grabbed onto each other, River's casted arm pulling Talon close. He didn't think it was possible, but this kiss was even better than the others.

Talon breathed his desire on frosty breaths in the moments between kisses. River let out a groan and pulled Talon closer against him. Then River's hand was on him, on the outside of his jeans. Talon's breath caught and deepened.

"God, you're gorgeous," River whispered, reaching to unbutton Talon's jeans.

He grabbed River's hand, stopping him. "Wait." His voice was thick and deep.

"What's wrong?" River asked.

It was embarrassing to say out loud. Scary too. His heart thudded hard against his ribs "I, um, I—well I haven't exactly—

you know—been with a guy." He hoped the semi-darkness hid his burning face.

River didn't seem fazed. "I kind of figured you hadn't, with living in a small town and not being out. I bet you had girlfriends though."

Talon's face burned hotter. He felt like a sellout. "Yeah," he mumbled.

"Are you a virgin?"

Talon shook his head. He'd slept with his last girlfriend. He wished he hadn't because it was only to cover his ass so that no one could entertain the fact that he might be gay. It made him feel like an ass and a hypocrite.

"Have you been with a lot of guys?" Talon asked.

"Enough." There seemed to be shame and sorrow and regret within the breadth of that word. River reached out and took Talon's hand. "You know we don't have to…not yet, if you don't want to."

Talon wanted to, but it scared him. "What's it like?"

"You want the truth?"

"Yeah."

River paused for a moment, then said, "It hurts at first, even if the person you're with gives a shit about you." He shook his head. "My first time was with some trucker I hitched a ride with. He didn't give two fucks about me or how much it hurt."

"I'm sorry."

River shrugged. "I've met some other people who weren't as bad, who at least cared a little. Had some real assholes too.

Sure as hell never found love though. Most guys I met just wanted a fuck or a blow job."

The things River said made Talon sick. He wished he could take away the pain that lived in River's voice. "Doesn't anybody want love?" he asked.

River laughed. "You're a real romantic, aren't you?"

Embarrassed, Talon tried to pull away, but River squeezed his hand. "It's okay," River said. "Ash always gives me shit about being too much of a romantic. Says it's not realistic."

Talon looked at the ground. "What's so wrong with love?"

"Nothing," River sighed. "I just don't know if most people find it."

Talon wanted to know if River thought they could find love, but he couldn't ask something like that. Not right now. Talking about sex would be easier. His mouth went dry and his heart pounded as loud as the drums in the forest. "You, um— you said we didn't have to sleep together, but, well, what if I want to?"

River squeezed his hand again. "I just don't think we should. Not right now. I don't want to do anything to hurt you." He turned and grinned at Talon. "But there are other things we can do." He took Talon's face in his hands and kissed him, pulling him close again.

They lay down and pulled the sleeping bag over them for warmth. River straddled Talon and pulled off his T-shirt and sweatshirt, kissing his chest, then worked his way down to Talon's stomach to just above the button on his jeans.

River tried to undo the button and zipper, but his cast kept getting in the way. Talon reached down and helped him. Then River's mouth was on him, warm and wet and beautiful.

He'd gotten blow jobs and hand jobs before. Every time he fantasized it was some gorgeous actor. Now he didn't have to fantasize. Now it was real…beautifully, incredibly real. In that moment, he became the darkness and the dawn, the thrumming heartbeat of the forest, the voices calling, "We love you!" And when it pulsed through him and poured out of him, he was finally free.

He was him.

He was.

When it was over, River lay beside him and held onto him.

He wanted to tell River what he'd done for him, but words weren't enough. The only thing he knew how to do was to kiss him, to try to show River how he felt. Before he could kiss River, River's fingers touched the raised marks on Talon's back. Talon flinched at the memories it evoked.

River sat up. "What happened to you?" he demanded. "Who the hell did that to you?"

Talon sat up too, but couldn't meet River's eyes. "My dad. After he saw us in the park."

"Fuck!" River's shoulders slumped and he hit the ground with his fist. "I'm sorry, man. It's my fault."

Talon grabbed River's hand. "Yeah? Well then it's my fault you got the shit beat out of you, my fault you got stabbed."

River shook his head. "I'm the one who came on to you. If I hadn't—"

"Shut up," Talon's eyes stung. "If you hadn't—if we hadn't kissed that night, I never would have run away. I, I'd probably be dead."

River's eyes went to the bandages on Talon's wrist and forearm, probably seeing it for the first time. His fingers brushed the edge of the bandage. "What did you do?" he asked, his voice shaking.

"It was stupid, I wasn't thinking straight." He told River how exhausted he'd been, how hopeless things seemed that night, how he'd been thinking about doing it for a while. Then he told River about Coyote Joe and Maddy and Duncan, and all the other people he'd met who'd helped him, who gave him shelter and friendship.

"I've been there, in that hopeless place," River said. "A few times. Sometimes the world really sucks, or at least the people in it suck."

"Yeah," Talon whispered, "like the people who did that to you." He nodded at River's cast.

"It was your buddy from the gas station and some of his friends."

"Fucking asshole!" Talon wished Luke was in front of him so he could beat the shit out of him.

River shrugged. "It's happened before. Different towns, same kind of people."

Talon's face burned. "If I ever see the asshole again, I'll kill him."

River put his hand on Talon's shoulder. "He's not worth it. People like him aren't gonna change."

"Was he the one who stabbed you?" Talon pictured the hunting knife Luke liked to carry with him.

River didn't answer, which gave Talon his answer.

"Can I see it?" Talon asked.

River slowly pulled his shirt and jacket up. The bandage that was supposed to cover the wound had shifted, revealing a line of stitches about four inches long. Talon reached out and touched River's stomach, just a few inches from the wound. "I want to make it better," he said in a soft voice. "I wish I could take it away." He kissed River and lay down with him. Then he kissed each bruise, each scrape he saw, careful not to touch the stitches. With each kiss, River's breath deepened.

Everything about River was intoxicating. His lean body, the sound of his breath, the way he looked at Talon when Talon undressed him. To reciprocate, to give pleasure and love back to someone who'd given him life, was just as intense as being on the receiving end. Somehow this person he'd only known for hours knew more about him than the people who'd known Talon his whole life.

"You're beautiful," Talon whispered as he settled in next to River and pulled the sleeping bag back over them again.

River let out a soft laugh. "No one's ever called me that before."

"I'm sorry—I didn't mean—"

River put his finger on Talon's lips. "I like it. I don't get it, but I like it."

"What do you mean?"

River ran his fingers over Talon's cheek. "I mean you're fucking gorgeous, probably homecoming king or some shit like that. So why me—some skinny street kid? I'm nothing."

Talon grabbed his face. "No, I was nothing. My whole life was a lie. One big fucked up shitty perfect lie of a life." He kissed River. "You're everything."

River chuckled. "Look at us, we're like some Hallmark movie."

Talon laughed too. "Nah, I don't think Hallmark does gay."

"They should." River let out a long yawn.

"You should get some rest."

River gave him a playful shove. "You should stop worrying about me."

Talon worked his fingers through River's messy brown hair. "Will you shut up and rest?"

##

Sunday, July 5

River slept most of the day. Talon stayed close to their camp. He'd wanted to talk to Maddy, but hadn't seen her all day. When he asked Duncan about her, Duncan gave him a vague answer about Maddy being tired from being up so late. Talon sensed there was more going on.

219

But Maddy was there when he and River went to the Main Meadow for supper. He'd probably worried for nothing. She seemed to be doing okay. It was nice to introduce River to Coyote Joe and everyone else who'd helped him since he'd gotten to the gathering. Ash was there too. She'd moved her stuff and set up camp near them.

That night, Kita and Nate built a fire in their little neighborhood of the gathering. The warmth and companionship made Talon feel like he'd come home.

"Where's everyone going after the gathering's over?" Kita asked.

It was something Talon didn't like to think about. Right here in this moment, things were better than good, but thinking about the end of the gathering left him feeling lost. It was hard to imagine not seeing most of these people again.

Talon wasn't the only one who seemed to feel sad, hesitant. No one answered right away. Duncan looked at Maddy, who looked away from him. Ash gave River a questioning look which made Talon worry. He had no idea what Ash and River's plans were. He and River hadn't talked about life beyond the gathering or if they'd even be together.

Rain and Campbell were the first ones to break the silence. "We've been talking," Rain said, nodding at Campbell. "It's a long story, but my mom died a few weeks ago." She swallowed and looked at the sky.

Talon didn't know what to say. Anything he thought of sounded cliche, and he didn't feel like he knew Rain or Campbell very well. They'd been nice to him, but he'd talked more to Kita and Nate, and a lot more to Maddy and Duncan.

Campbell put his arm around Rain which seemed to give her the strength to talk again. "My mom has a beautiful place near Durango, Colorado—a house that's off the grid, lots of organic gardens, some chickens and goats and horses. She, um, she…" Her voice broke for a moment, then she gathered herself. "She always helped anyone who needed it. When I was a kid, it was animals. And I guess the last ten years or so, she'd been helping people, giving them food and a place to stay in exchange for help with the land and the animals." She looked at Campbell. "We both want to continue her work, but in a bigger way if we can."

Campbell nodded. "Your mom would love that you're doing this."

"She would," Rain said. "I think coming here, meeting all of you, it's helped me remember what's really important, and it's helped me finally figure out what I want to do with my life, to finally find some meaning in the work I do." She took a breath. "We want to add on to my mom's house and build a couple of cabins too. It can be there for whoever needs a place to stay for a while—for however long they need it. We just ask that people give as much back as they can by pitching in with construction or with the animals or gardens. Even though I'm an architect and Campbell's a contractor, we could use all the help we can get."

Rain looked at Talon, making him wonder what she was thinking.

"You're the one who gave me the idea. You and Kita."

Kita looked just as surprised as Talon felt. "Why me?" he asked.

Recognition settled across Kita's face. "I told Rain I was glad I could help you, even if it was something as simple as giving you my tent and sleeping bag. I haven't always done the greatest job helping my daughter, but I was glad I could do something for you."

"And then we wondered where you'd go after the gathering," Rain said. "That's when I had the idea for my mom's place. So I guess what I'm saying is that you have a place to stay if you need it, for as long as you need it. That goes for all of you."

Talon had no idea what to say. He didn't think Rain or any of them would give him a second thought once the gathering was over. He looked around the group. Coyote Joe looked deep in thought. Duncan gave Maddy a hopeful look and squeezed her hand. Instead of returning the look, she got up and walked away. Kita looked like she was about to follow Maddy, but Duncan held up his hand. "Just give her some time," he said, sounding defeated.

Talon sat in the silence, not knowing how to respond. He wanted to know what was wrong with Maddy. He wanted to know what River and Ash were thinking. He wanted to hug Kita and Rain for thinking of him, for wanting to help him.

"I'm sorry," Rain said when his silence stretched on for too long. "I came on too strong. It's all the years I lived in New York. It was just an idea. No one has to come, it was just—"

"It sounds real nice," Coyote Joe said. "Nicer than anything I've heard in a while. Count me in if you don't mind my old arthritic hands. It might be nice to be a part of something again."

Campbell reached over and clapped Coyote Joe on the back. "We'd be honored to have you."

Nate and Kita whispered back and forth for a few minutes while Talon still struggled for something to say.

"We can give a ride to anyone who wants to come and help you," Nate said. "There's plenty of room on my bus."

Campbell looked surprised. "I thought you two were on your way to California."

"We are," Kita said, "but we can take a detour. California will still be there in a few weeks or a few months." She turned to Talon, who was just a few feet away. "You could ride with us—all of you—if you want to."

"I—I don't know what I'm doing," Talon stammered. "Or what they're doing." He nodded at Ash and River.

River looked away as soon as Talon said the last words. He'd thought he was giving River space by saying it. He didn't want River to feel pressured into staying with him.

River followed in Maddy's footsteps by getting up and taking off toward the main trail.

Talon glanced at Rain, who looked heartbroken, like she'd caused Maddy and River to leave. "I need to go find him," Talon said. He looked at Rain, wanting her to know how much her offer meant to him. "Thanks, Rain. I mean it."

Talon found River inside the tent they'd shared. He was stuffing some clothes in his backpack, and barely looked up when Talon came inside.

"What did I do?" Talon asked, his eyes burning. "What happened back there? What's wrong?"

River whipped his head around to look at Talon, his eyes cold. "I don't get you. One minute I think you might actually care about me. The next minute me and Ash are *them*—'I don't know what *they're* doing' like we barely mean shit to you, like we're separate from you. What the hell am I supposed to think?"

Talon sat down and clenched his fists, tired of trying to figure out the right thing to say. All it did was backfire on him. "I don't know what you're supposed to think. Hell, what am I supposed to think?" he threw back at River. "You and Ash have this bond, and you and I—we just met. You're this free spirit who just goes wherever. Maybe you don't want me tagging along like a puppy."

River held Talon's sweatshirt in his hands, kneading it into a ball. "Did you ever think that me and Ash *go wherever* because we don't have anywhere to go? We don't have a fucking choice! Nobody wants us. Until now." He hung his head. "At least I thought somebody wanted us. Wanted me."

Talon scooted closer to River so he was directly across from him. He reached out and stilled River's hands. "River," he said, trying to draw River's eyes to him. "I want you more than I've ever wanted anything."

"You mean it?" he said in a soft voice.

Talon leaned forward and kissed him. River let go of the sweatshirt and pulled Talon to him. They fell onto the pile of sleeping bags, and Talon lost himself in Rivers arms, his mouth, his hands, his body.

##

It was the freezing part of the late night/early morning when Talon went outside to go to the bathroom. He almost tripped over Duncan's feet. Talon hadn't seen him sitting against a nearby tree.

"Sorry," Talon said. He looked around for Maddy but didn't see her.

"Don't worry about it," Duncan said, sounding dejected. He shoved his hands in his winter coat pockets.

Talon shivered, wishing he had more clothes with him. Between Campbell and Nate and Duncan, they'd lent him enough so he could at least wear enough layers not to freeze.

"You okay?" Talon asked. He thought by now Maddy and Duncan would have worked out whatever was going on between them. They seemed close, the kind of close that couldn't be broken.

Duncan shrugged. "I guess. It's nothing for you to worry about."

He was worried. "Is Maddy okay?"

Duncan looked at the ground and mumbled, "That's not for me to say."

He wanted to reach out to Duncan, but stopped himself. "You sure you're okay?"

Duncan gave him a rueful smile that showed in the dull light of Talon's little flashlight. "You're a pretty smart kid."

"Maddy's one in a million, isn't she," Talon said.

Duncan nodded. "More like one in a billion."

Talon sat beside Duncan. "Have you known her very long?"

"Not long enough." He sighed and hung his head. "It won't ever be long enough—for me anyway. I don't know about her."

"But she'll be back, right?" Talon couldn't imagine not seeing her again.

"Yeah. She wouldn't leave without knowing you and River were okay first."

"Well, she won't leave without you either."

Duncan shook his head. "I'm not so sure about that."

Talon wished he could think of something to say to make Duncan feel better. He and Maddy had gone way out of their way to help him, even risking being arrested by police. But it didn't seem like anything could cheer Duncan up at that moment. "You want me to hang out with you for a while?"

"No." Duncan tried to sound light-hearted, but it didn't work. "You should get back to your tent so you don't freeze.

River stirred when Talon lay beside him and snuggled close behind him. "River?"

"Hmmm?" he said in a sleepy voice.

"Will you go to Rain's place with me after the gathering. I mean if Ash wants to go too?"

"Yeah. Ash will want to go. She doesn't like the road."

"Okay."

Talon wanted to talk to River about Maddy and Duncan, but from the sound of River's breathing, he was already asleep again.

Despite everything good that had happened, Talon couldn't sleep. Something was going on with Maddy and he couldn't stand not knowing what. In just a short time, she'd become one of the most important people in his life.

He must have eventually dosed off but woke to Duncan and Maddy's voices not far from his tent.

"I know you're trying to ignore it, but you're worn out, Maddy. It's not going to hurt to take a little break, to go to Durango. Just for a little while. Not forever."

"I can't." She sounded almost panicked. "There are still too many places I want to go, places I need to go."

"I know, but you can still go to those places after you have time to catch your breath," Duncan said.

"I can't go to Rain's place. I have to keep moving."

"Even if it's wearing you down?" Duncan asked, sounding frustrated.

"I'm not magically going to get better if I rest," she spat. "I don't have the flu—its not something I'm going to get over!"

Talon's stomach flipped and twisted into knots. He'd thought she was hiding something, but this sounded serious. Did she have cancer? The thought made him want to throw up.

"I know," Duncan said, sounding defeated. "I know it won't go away."

"That's why I can't stop."

"So you still want to leave after the gathering," Duncan said. "You want to go back to Boulder and get in your car and leave. No regrets?"

"That's not fair, Duncan. Of course I don't want to leave you, but I can't stay still." Her voice cracked. "I—I can't."

"Even just for a few weeks?"

"No," she said emphatically.

"Why?"

"Because I'm dying."

Talon sucked in a breath and put a hand to his chest. It couldn't be real. It had to be a mistake. She was too young, too healthy, too good of a person. Someone like her wasn't supposed to be dying. Talon wanted to go to her, to talk to her, but it wasn't his place. Not right now.

"Oh, god," she said, her voice breaking, "I'm gonna die, Duncan."

There was nothing after that, but the soft sounds of crying and whispered voices. Talon wrapped his hands around his stomach like someone had punched him.

For the next hour, Talon sat in the tent, hugging his knees, trying to rework the conversation he'd overheard, trying to make it mean something else. He wanted to wake River, to tell him, to seek comfort, but River was still exhausted and needed rest.

Finally, Talon couldn't take it anymore. He stepped outside, needing to breathe the frigid air, to see the rich canopy of stars that hung over all of them. When he left the tent, he saw Maddy in the moonlight sitting against the same tree where

Duncan had been, just a few feet away from where they'd had their fire earlier.

The sight of her made his eyes water. It was strange to feel so much, to love her after less than a week of knowing her, but he couldn't explain it any more than loving River the night they'd met.

He wanted to go to her, to hug her, to grieve with her, but he wasn't sure she'd let him. "Hey," he said, trying to sound casual.

She wiped her nose and tried to smile. "Hey. What are you doing up?"

He sat beside her, trying not to shiver. "Couldn't sleep."

"Me neither. She tossed part of her wool blanket over him. "You're going to freeze to death if you don't cover up."

The word *death* made him want to throw up. "Is it true?"

"What do you mean?"

He hung his head. "I'm sorry, I overheard you and Duncan. Are—are you really—dying?" His voice cracked on the last word.

"Oh, Talon," she sighed, sounding sadder for him than she was for herself. "I never meant for anyone to find out, especially you."

Her words scraped him raw. "Why me? You think I can't handle it?"

"You shouldn't have to handle it," she said with an edge to her voice. "No one should. Not you, not Duncan… Nobody."

He clenched his fists, needing to say it. "We love you and you're gonna have to deal with that, okay? And that means you're not gonna get rid of us." He swiped at the tears that felt like ice on his cheeks.

"God, where did you come from?" she choked, half laughing, half crying. "Some kid who shows up out of nowhere with nothing to his name." She reached over and ruffled his hair. "And you stole my heart, and everyone else who's met you."

He ground his heel into the cold dirt. "I'm nothin' special."

"But you are. You brought us all together."

He shook his head. "You already knew each other by the time I got here."

"I know, but you really brought us together. Everyone was going to leave and go their own way, but not now. I know it sounds corny, but I think all of us needed each other in some way or another."

"But we need you too." He hoped she heard the truth in his voice. "And maybe you need us? Just say you'll come, at least for a little while."

She turned her face to the sky and smiled at the scattering of brilliant lights. "How can I say no to that?"

He joined her in looking at the stars. The sight of them so brilliant, so bright made him think about everyone he'd met at the gathering. They were all like beautiful points of light, shining so bright they saved him. He was there in the stars too, finally able to shine because of them.

##

The gathering had officially ended, and twelve of them made the long hike to the parking area. During the hike, Kita pulled Talon aside. "Could you do something for me?" she asked.

"What?"

"I know your parents might not deserve it, but could you drop them a note or a letter just letting them know you're all right? You don't have to say anything else or tell them where you're going. We can mail it while we're still in Utah so they won't know where you're headed."

The welts on Talon's back were still so fresh it was hard to think about doing anything nice for his parents. "I don't—I mean—why should I?"

"I'm pretty sure my daughter hates me, and she probably should. If she took off, I'd give anything to know that she was okay. I'm not asking you to forgive them—just let them know you're okay."

His mind turned from his parents to Delphine. His parents didn't deserve peace of mind, but Delphine did. If Delphine chose to tell their parents she'd gotten a letter from him, she could. "I'll send a note to my sister."

Kita put her arm around him and gave his shoulder a squeeze. "Thank you."

They reached Nate's bus first. Nate, Kita, Coyote Joe, Talon, River, Ash, Sonny, and Ripple would follow Rain and Campbell to Durango. Maddy and Duncan were headed to Boulder to get Maddy's car, then they'd make the drive to

Durango. Even though they wouldn't be far behind, Talon didn't like leaving them.

"Promise you'll come," Talon said as he hugged Maddy.

"I promise."

River gave them each a quick hug, then he and Talon went to stand beside Nate's bus.

"You okay leaving home?" River asked. "Probably for good?"

There were things he'd miss about his family, but until they accepted him, he couldn't be there. "This was more home than anyplace I've ever been." He looked at everyone taking turns hugging Maddy and Duncan, then he took River's hand. "I think we were all looking for home, for family."

"You think we really found it?" The hint of doubt in River's voice showed Talon just how hard the world had been on him.

He turned to River and kissed him, trying to give him the answer. Talon held onto him even after the kiss was over. "Yeah, I do," he whispered.

There was so much that went into writing this book, and I never could have done it alone. A huge thank you to the team at Unsolicited Press for believing in my novel and for all your hard work in every step of the publishing process. Thank you to all my critique partners and beta readers from the Des Moines Writer's Workshop. This novel wouldn't be the same without your thoughtful feedback. A special thanks to Frani and Jo. Your enthusiasm for my characters and their stories pushed me to keep going even when I got discouraged.

Words cannot express my gratitude for my immediate family and my extended family for their ongoing encouragement (and patience when I'd lock myself away for hours to write). You all mean the world to me. A big shout out to my mom who has been my biggest cheerleader since I wrote my first story when I was five years old.

ABOUT THE AUTHOR

Beth Burgmeyer writes fiction and creative nonfiction. Her work has appeared in Ponder Review, The Ocotillo Review, Santa Clara Review, Miracle Monocle, and others. She won first place in the CIBA Somerset Awards for Literary and Contemporary Fiction and was a finalist in the Acacia Fiction Prize. Beth is a mental health counselor specializing in equine assisted psychotherapy. She lives near Des Moines, Iowa with her family and a menagerie of animals.

ABOUT THE PRESS

Unsolicited Press is based out of Portland, Oregon and focuses on the works of the unsung and underrepresented. As a womxn-owned, all-volunteer small publisher that doesn't worry about profits as much as championing exceptional literature, we have the privilege of partnering with authors skirting the fringes of the lit world. We've worked with emerging and award-winning authors such as Tara Stillions Whitehead, Heather Lang Cassera, Shann Ray, Amy Shimshon-Santo, Brook Bhagat, Kris Amos, and John W. Bateman.

Learn more at unsolicitedpress.com. Find us on twitter and instagram.